9009

JAMES HOPPER AND FRED R. BECHDOLT

HEATHEN EDITIONS
THEIR BOOKS. OUR WAY.

Published in the good ole United States of America
by Heathen Editions, an imprint of
Heathen Creative
P.O. Box 588
Point Pleasant, WV 25550-0588

Heathen Editions are available at quantity discounts.
For information and more tomfoolery, check us out online:

heatheneditions.com

@heatheneditions
#heathenedition

First serialized in *The Saturday Evening Post* 1908
"The Tracy–Merrill Escape" first published 1922
Heathen Edition published 2022

Book and cover design by Sheridan Cleland
Set in 11pt Plantin Std
Chapters in Deccan

ISBN: 978-1-948316-99-6

FIRST HEATHEN EDITION
1 2 3 4 5 6 7 8 9 0

"It is painfully realistic." —*The New York Times*

"Almost too terrible in its realism is the story of a convict '9009' by James Hopper and Fred R. Bechdolt. It is the kind of story which makes the reader on fire against the injustice of justice."
—The Graphic

"Put into commonplace language, without hysteria, it is a protest against the American penal system."
—The Saturday Review

"Very real, very dramatic, and most tragical in its ending."
—The Book News Monthly

"Achieves a bone-chilling effect by consistently using '9009' as the name of the protagonist."
—H. Bruce Franklin, *Prison Literature in America*

"From cover to cover, a book of horror and grim, relentless realism. A fact-story, **9009** might have been a collaboration of Poe, Hugo, and Oscar Wilde." *—Sunset*

"The book is the heaviest blow that has been struck the prison system since Oscar Wilde's *The Ballad of Reading Gaol*."
—Newark Call

"A story of prison life, authentic as to fact, that will prove a great sensation in its startling revelation of the present management of prisons." *—The Publishers' Weekly*

"A book decidedly out of the ordinary . . . a remarkable story. It is an intricate psychological study of an imprisoned man and an appalling indictment of our prison systems. Aside from the artistic value of the book, the sweep of the facts which it presents is staggering. As has been well said, '9009' is a question which must be answered."
—Janet B. McGovern, *The Los Angeles Times*

TO
ONE WHO WEPT

Heathenry:
Thoughts on the Text

What a book! This thing simmers until it explodes, and when it does—*watch out*. It's credited to two authors—James Hopper and Fred R. Bechdolt—but research has led us to agree with H. L. Mencken:[1] Hopper was likely the author, with Bechdolt supplying the facts.

What immediately stands out is Hopper's lean, stripped-down writing style. There is no fat on this thing: it's brisk, brash, and brutal. Need more alliteration? It's also electric, economical, and efficient. We Heathens are big fans of Donald E. Westlake's *Parker* series that he penned as Richard Stark, and Hopper feels very much like a precursor—emphasis on the *stark*. Westlake kicked around in that noir, antihero sandbox made popular by the likes of Raymond Chandler and Dashiell Hammett, but this book is proof Hopper was building a sandcastle there long before they arrived—which is to say *9009* was pulp *before* there was pulp.

At the same time, though, it's a scathing indictment of the American penal system as it existed at the turn of the 20th century. In their preface, Hopper and Bechdolt make it clear that everything that happens in *9009* is "something

[1] See footnote on the following page.

which has happened to some convict in some prison some time." While that statement may sound engineered in order to lend their novel some based-on-fact validity, we Heathens are knee-deep in production on a whole gaggle of autobiographies/prison reform books authored by Donald Lowrie, Thomas Mott Osborne, Ed Morrell, and Jack Black, among others (we're calling it our Convictions series), and we can emphatically state that when they say it's based in truth—*we believe them*. Lowrie's first book, *My Life in Prison*, is full to the brim with prison absurdities. Then, Morrell sees his absurdities and raises him several insanities in his own *The 25th Man*. Jennings, this story's antagonist, could easily be a real-life character in either of their books.

But, maybe it's not enough for them to say it's based on facts and for us to say we believe them. We can hear the challenge now: *where's the proof?*

You want proof?

We've got proof.

9009 borrows many of its elements from the prison break perpetrated by Harry Tracy (prisoner #4088) and David Merrill (#4089) from the Oregon State Penitentiary on June 9th, 1902. And rather than expound on the similarities and spoil *both* stories for you, we have included an account of that escape (with images)—as detailed in the book *Sensational Prison Escapes From The Oregon State Penitentiary* published in 1922 by Prisoner #6435—so you can draw your own conclusions on what is fact and what is fiction.

As for the text, we've kept our Heathening to the bare minimum given how modern Hopper's writing reads as-is. The only modifications we've made have been in updating a few words to their current equivalents (e.g. cell-mate is now cellmate, shot-gun is now shotgun, etc.), which we're pleased to report makes this ripping tale rip *faster*.

Ready?

Go!

0000

The impulse which moved us to write this book was primarily indignation—indignation at facts. At facts learned slowly and gradually by one of us through years of patient investigation, and then told, all in one mass, to the other, who thus came to them with an abruptness giving intense vision.[1] A work written in the fervor of indignation is apt to be violent, unbalanced, and unjust. We were alive to this danger; after some thought, we saw how we could best avoid it. It was by using in the story facts only. *9009* is a story made of facts—a Fact-Story.

By this we do not mean that *9009* is a biography. Convict 9009—John Collins—exists only in our imagination. But everything that happens to 9009 within the prison is something which has happened to some convict in some prison (American prison) some time. And much worse things could have happened to 9009. By which we mean that much worse things have happened to some convicts in some prisons sometimes—and we know of these things.

So that, besides sticking to truth in writing the story of

---

[1] H. L. Mencken (1880–1956) in his review of *9009* for *The Smart Set* (February 1909 – Vol. 27, No. 2 – p. 155) stated: "Judging by certain correspondence recently appearing in the literary gazettes I fancy that Bechdolt furnished the facts and Hopper wrote the story."

9009, we have done more. We have eliminated what was too terrible about this truth, and in the expression of that which we have divulged we have used repression. The result, we think, is a simple, clear, compressed story, all of action, which shows how Society creates a Monster. How Society through sheer, crass stupidity, creates a Monster, which then it has to destroy (stupidly) at the cost of labor, blood, and (which may concern it more) of much gold.

0001

John Collins sat upon the lurching bench of the wagon, his right wrist linked to a garroter,[1] his left wrist linked to a murderer; his eyes were straining for the first sight of the thing he feared. Before him, on the front seat, the sheriff gossiped lazily to the driver, who idly flicked the lash of his whip across the horses' sweating flanks. Behind, upon the back seat, the two deputies watched with sawed-off shotguns across their knees. The wagon rolled slowly, with sudden creaking pitchings, along a dust-heaped road which coiled its way to the summit of a tawny hill. To the east, far down, white flecks danced upon the bay's green waters, and from the shore breaths of wind came gliding up through the dry wild oats in long silvery undulations.

The horses gained the level and broke into a trot; the carriage plunged forward and down—and a gray wall leaped up from the ground against the sky. The murderer sucked in a whistling breath. The wall rose as they approached; it hung over them, gray and ponderous, turreted as a medieval battlement. The garroter laughed, a harsh braggart laugh, and pointed, raising with his arm Collins' coupled wrist. But Collins leaned forward unheeding, staring silently.

The wagon, drawing a smooth ellipse, was coming up to a

---

[1] One who strangles in order to commit robbery.

brick building which jutted out like a buttress from the center of the wall; two steel-barred gates swung themselves open as of their own volition as the prisoners alighted. Flanked by the murderer and the garroter, the sheriff before him, the deputies behind, John Collins walked in. A voice spoke overhead; a blue-sleeved arm emerged from a window and drooped downward, dangling a large iron key at the end of its stumpy fingers; from a stone bench at the entrance a stripes-clad man rose, took the key, and locked the gate. Officers and felons now stood in an arched passageway which smelled damp, like a tunnel. They were within, but Collins hardly noted the fact; he had turned his head and was watching the stripes-clad man.

He was the first convict that John Collins had ever seen. He wore a two-piece garment, coarse shoes, and a visored cap. Jacket and trousers were circled by alternating bars of black and white; the cap was similarly barred from back to front. But it was not the garment that drew the attention of John Collins. It was the man's face. There was something about it—it may have been in the bloodless cheeks—something arsenical and poisonous; something glittering, too—it may have been in the eyes—something glittering, furtive, and threatening. Collins could not fathom the look, but a vague discomfort slid coldly along his spine.

Walking beneath the concrete arch, between the garroter and the murderer, linked to them with steel, he passed from beneath the spanning building into a court. On the right were several doors; at the second one was a narrow bench upon which they sat, while the sheriff unlocked the cuffs from their wrists and then with his deputies entered the turnkey's office.[2] The murderer was breathing thickly, like a man asleep. The garroter was silent for a moment. Then he stretched forth his arms rubbing his wrists with his hands, and laughed harshly.

"Same old mill!" he cried; and then, in a jeering voice to

---

[2] A turnkey is the person in charge of the keys of a prison; jailer.

Collins, "Yes, take yer gapins now, you rum; ye'll see enough of it before ye're done with it!"

John Collins was looking about him. His eyes fell upon a little garden in the center of the court. A fountain was playing upon red flowers. But he was still pondering on the expression of the convict of the gate. He could not forget the look, and he could not explain it. It was a look bearing fear, and giving fear. It was the look of a rat. A rat! That was it. A look such as one gets from a rat in a dusky corner.

The murderer was staring dully, past the red flowers and the jetting water which he did not see, staring at the gray walls beyond which he would never pass again. Along the summit of the wall a blue-clad man was pacing slowly, sharply silhouetted; he held in his right hand a rifle, carrying it loosely, like a hunter. The garroter leaned and grinned into the murderer's face.

"You'll wish they'd handed you the book and you'd been hung," he snarled; "you'll wish that more'n once before ye've croaked in this mill!" But the other did not seem to hear. Collins, though there was little softness in his heart, felt an uneasiness at the creaking cruelty of the words. His eyes went up and away across the enclosure to a high stone building with top-floor windows heavily barred.

"Them's the condemned cells up there on top," went on the garroter, noting the direction of Collins' glance—and then, to the murderer: "You'll live there, pal."

But the murderer still stared at the stretch of high stone wall, with its pacing guard holding his gun loosely, like a hunter.

A man was coming toward them, across the garden. He was squarely, brutally built, was clad in blue, wore a white felt hat, jauntily creased, and as he passed cut at a flower with his light rattan[3] cane. As he drew close Collins saw his face, yellow-brown; and set in this yellow-brown face, two eyes,

---

[3] The stem of various climbing palm trees used to make wickerwork, furniture, and canes.

ch. ends next p.

white-gray, opaque, without light; two eyes hard like metal. Furtively the garroter bent his head; he coughed behind his hand, which had risen to hide his face. The man stopped, glanced sharply down upon him, then seized the upraised hand, jerking it roughly from the face. His white-gray eyes set themselves stonily into those of the thug, which immediately escaped to the right, then to the left, then to the ground. The blue-clad man laughed silently.

"So you're back, eh, Thurston?" he said. He spoke lightly, and his heavy sallow face showed no emotion; yet into it, bending downward on the bowed head of the other, there seemed to creep, somehow, a dull menace. "Back again," he repeated musingly; "and you thought I wasn't going to make you!" He chuckled with little sound. "I know a friend that's here, a-waiting to see you; a good friend—ain't you glad he's still here, eh?" There was some deadly meaning to the words. Collins saw the garroter shrivel beneath them. Then the man was staring at him. John Collins stared back, as it was his habit to do. The eyes met; John Collins felt the gray ones, round, almost lidless, boring into him without emotion, without trace of human feeling; he struggled; in spite of himself he felt the defiant challenge flicker in his own, flicker, almost go out; he threw back his head then the other had pivoted on his heels and, cutting the air in a whistling stroke of his rattan cane, had passed into the turnkey's office.

The garroter muttered an oath and slowly raised his white face. "Who is that?" asked John Collins.

"Jennings—one of the jute-mill guards," answered the thug; "look out fer him." He spoke almost in a whisper and lapsed silent at once.

The sheriff and his deputies were leaving. The sheriff shook hands with the murderer and the garroter. "Goodbye, boys," he said; "do the best you can for yourselves." He turned to John Collins. "It's your first time," he said: "remember and keep to yourself. Keep to yourself and hang on to your good-time; hang on to your copper." He hurried on after the others. John Collins' eyes followed the three men into the dark vaulted way. Suddenly the tunnel was lit up as with a burst of golden light; at its extremity, roundly framed, appeared the outline of a hill, tawny against a blue sky.

There was a metallic clang; the tunnel darkened again. Collins' eyes turned back to the gray walls. "Hang on to your copper," he murmured vaguely.[4]

---

[4] According to *Green's Dictionary of Slang*, the use of "copper" to mean "good conduct marks" for prisoners originated (in print) with this very book in 1908.

0002

For some time the three sat silent on the bench before the garden, with its fountain playing upon the red flowers. The garroter's head, now, was bent like the murderer's, and he was muttering to himself. He straightened suddenly, touching Collins' elbow with his hand.

"Listen, pal," he said hoarsely; "I'll wise you to a thing or two." His thick lips trembled loosely. "It's the cons; watch them. The cons"—he looked up into Collins' face almost appealingly, as though begging permission to rid himself of a weight. "The guards—they're bad enough; God knows they're all bad in this hell-hole. But the cons—they're devils." His grip upon Collins' elbow tightened. "Every wan of them's ready to give ye the worst of it some way, to job ye if he can; every wan of them is stoolin' on the other"—he gulped oddly, seemed to swallow three or four times with the motion of a bird drinking—"or lookin' to kill ye because he thinks ye've stooled on him!" he finished with sudden passion.

A stripes-clad man was coming out of the turnkey's office. "The bath-trusty"[1] whispered the garroter, immediately resuming his cringing posture; "he's come for us." The bath-trusty was dressed as the man Collins had seen at the gate, but his hair, instead of being cropped close, like the other's,

---

[1] A trusty is a prisoner considered trustworthy and allowed special privileges.

was of medium length. He was scanning a slip of paper in his hand, and in his sharp face, bent to read, Collins fancied he saw the shadow of what he had seen in the face of the convict by the gate. As the man looked up at him, the impression was confirmed. The man had rat eyes.

He waved his hand to them authoritatively. "Come on," he said, and turned his back. They followed, the garroter first, and behind John Collins, the murderer, still silent, as though dazed. They went through a hallway and up an iron flight of stairs to a room into which warm rays of sun slanted through a skylight. Here another convict received them pointing, without giving them a glance, to a bench upon which they sat while he turned to adjust the lens of a large camera. He wore green eye-shades instead of the visored cap; his black hair was quite long and foppishly parted; a little mustache covered his upper lip; his striped jacket was rounded at the bottom and had lapels; his striped trousers were carefully creased, and his buttoned shoes were of glistening patent leather. Also he wore a white collar and a four-in-hand tie. His forehead was low beneath the shiny black bangs, and there was something venomously alert about his slight body and beady eyes.

By this man and the bath-trusty few words were exchanged, and these obviously restricted to the business at hand. Between them was a barrier of caste: the photographer treated the bath-trusty with the same authority of word and manner which the latter used toward the three prisoners. And yet, through this barrier, something was constantly passing—sometimes in half-averted head, and often in sharp sidelong glance from narrowed eye—something that showed that the high standing of the one did not put him beyond peril from the other; there was not a moment when the two were not watching each other furtively. They watched each other like two hungry cats; it was as though the photographer were a cat holding a bleeding piece of meat and the other were waiting for him to slacken his guard for just a moment.

One thing was plain: there was absolutely no community of interest between the two convicts; no need of guards to watch while the two were together. All of which impressed Collins vaguely, as he sat for his picture, first bare-headed, then with his hat on.

After which the three followed the bath-trusty to an inner room in which incandescent lights glowed yellow between shelves and drawers that lined the walls. At the order of another stripes-clad man, the three stripped naked in the room. Leaving their clothes there, they crossed the hall and spent ten minutes in a large concrete tank, scrubbing themselves with coarse brown soap and warm water. They returned. The bath-trusty consulted with the trusty of the clothes room. Again Collins saw the sidelong looks from narrowed eyes, the incessant watching, and then the clothes-room trusty measured the three loosely. He was a bent little man, hollow-cheeked; his eyes roved, shifting from place to place like the sun gleam from a mirror in a boy's hand; but always they flitted back to the bath-trusty. And the bath-trusty, in turn, watched him far more closely than he watched his three charges.

They were standing stark while the clothes-room trusty rummaged about shelves and drawers and made notes in an account book. Finally, he placed before each a little pile of clothing—underwear, a striped suit, a barred cap, and a pair of coarse lace shoes. On the back of each jacket, at the collar, was a square of white cloth, and on each square the bent little convict stamped in purple ink a number. Collins, picking up his jacket, looked at the number. He was 9009.

He slid on the garments silently; and as their coarseness rasped his skin, as their ugly bars gloomed in his eyes, there came to him a feeling which the stone walls, the hardness of the garroter, the rat eyes of the trusties, the harsh implacability of walls and men, had not yet given him. As he stepped from the chair of the prison barber, his face smooth-shaven, his hair cropped close, this feeling took on a character of

ch. ends p. 12

finality. So it was with the other two. Into each face had come a heaviness, a blank hopelessness; lines had sprung that added years to age, that took away whatever flicker had remained of gentleness and youth. The pictures now taken were as of other men than those who posed before. Even the murderer had changed.

The summer sun had sunk behind the surrounding walls as they, each with a roll of bedding upon his shoulder, stepped out again into the court, after having been pawed lightly by the photographer, measuring them by the Bertillon system.[2] They left the murderer at the heavily barred stone building to which the garroter had prophetically pointed; and 9009 and the garroter followed the bath-trusty till they came to a large open space. This was flanked by two cell houses, a number of smaller buildings, and a stretch of high stone wall. The cell houses, with their long rows of black-barred windows, frowned down upon this space which, although large, seemed crushingly close, and the earth of which was beaten by feet into cement-like hardness. Along the top of the wall two blue-clad men were slowly walking, approaching a corner which was capped by a box like a tower. Each carried in his right hand a rifle, loosely, like a hunter. In the wall, near the cell house was a great steel-barred gate, and over this was an open turret from which protruded the vicious muzzle of a rapid-fire gun. Here two more blue-clad guards stood with rifles.

As 9009, the garroter, and the trusty reached the center of the yard, the gates in the wall suddenly swung inward with a clang, and through the arched way, beneath the turret with its rapid-fire gun, a line of convicts began to flow inward, a line writhing like a snake, gray as a larva, and mounted upon

[2] Alphonse Bertillon (1853–1914) was a French police officer and criminologist who applied the anthropological technique of anthropometry (the measurement of a human) to law enforcement creating an identification system, known as the Bertillon System, based on physical measurements. It was the first scientific system used by police to identify criminals until superseded by the technique of fingerprinting at the beginning of the 20th century.

legs like a centipede. It came, slowly, smoothly, across the yard, toward 9009, the garroter, and the trusty, who had halted; it crept by them; its head sank into the door of one of the cell houses to the right; and still the tail was oozing, as though it were to be endlessly, out of the archway to the left. 9009 understood; it was the lockstep of which he often had heard. The convicts marched in single file, each with both hands on the shoulders of the man before him; from this came the undulating unison of the long, striped thing. It crawled by him; he scanned its links; one by one the white faces flashed by. Each face was set straight ahead, looking downward; each face was white and held a dull hardness. And from these men, each touching the other with both hands on his shoulders, there came no sound; the lips were motionless. They marched; from head to tail the monster undulated smoothly. They marched, eyes to the ground, and grimly silent. And the stripes of all were black and gray, black and gray, black and gray—until a startling change in the ringed line's length struck 9009 almost like a blow. It was a convict clad in stripes of black and red.

9009 heard, at his elbow, the sound of breath sucked sharply in; the garroter, leaning forward with yellow face, was watching the red-striped convict.

He came on, linked in front by his own arms, linked behind by the arms of another, a red blotch in the long gray line, till even with them. He marched with head bowed and shoulders bent. His face was dead-white with the prison pallor, heavy-jawed, and a scowl like a corrosion cleft his forehead; his eyes scanned the ground at his feet.

The garroter swallowed hard, his knees bent a bit and his shoulders rose a little; and then, suddenly, as if drawn by this shrinking movement, the eyes of the red-striped man left the ground and lit upon him. It was a flash, a glance in passing, a flicker of the lids, and the eyes went back to the beaten ground; but in that instant there had leaped from the pallid face, coarse-mouthed, a look so eloquent of hate, so

ch. ends next p.

dire of promise, a look a-shout with such ferocious joy, that 9009 himself went cold. The garroter was livid, and drops of sweat stood out upon his forehead.

"My God!" he said thickly.

The bath-trusty, looking straight ahead as though he were not talking, said: "He cut Donnely just after you left and got another twenty. He's just out of solitary; first day in the jute."

"I didn't stool," muttered the garroter—and his muttering, though low, had the inflection of a wail. "I didn't stool."

The trusty marched them on; a minute later 9009 was in his cell.

0003

The next morning, 9009 was awakened by a rude hand and taken to the yard captain's office to be booked. A keen-eyed, iron-gray man met him there and, after stripping him, scanned his bare body inch by inch for scars.

He examined first the face of 9009, passing his eyes slowly and mercilessly over each feature, exploring every fold and pit of skin; then, with the same passionless, peering scrutiny, like that of an old woman examining a piece of meat at the market, he searched the arms, the hands, the naked torso, and finally the feet. At times he stopped and marked down the result of his observation into a little notebook. When he was through, he had not spoken a word; he had not seen the man.

Having slipped on his garments again, 9009 stood a moment awkwardly in the center of the room, not knowing what was expected of him, and unconsciously watching the clerk book his commitment: "John Collins, Union County, July 19, 1897; Burglary and Assault to Commit Murder; five years and three years."

The clerk was young and slender, clad in blue; his boyish lips curved in a vague smile. The book was thick, heavy, its large page ruled off by vertical lines of red and blue. The pen scratched and sputtered. The clerk stopped and replaced it with another, then went on writing, smiling vaguely into the book.

"Five years and three years."

9009 dropped his eyes to the floor; it was concrete, hard, like stone. He raised his eyes to the window; it was steel-barred. Through the squares he saw a stretch of wall; on the top, cutting the sky in silhouette, a guard paced slowly, carrying his rifle in his hand, loosely, like a hunter.

"Five years and three years. Eight years," thought 9009.

A sudden report, sharp and loud as a pistol-shot, made him jump. The clerk had slammed the book shut.

The rat-eyed trusty was standing in the doorway, beckoning. 9009 followed him across the yard into the cell-house, up two flights of iron stairs, along a narrow steel platform, past a long row of steel-barred doors, back to his cell. Following the prison regulations he must pass his first day in his cell.

The night before, he had thrown his bedding upon the narrow bunk and, stretching upon it, had immediately sunk into a brutish sleep. Now he looked about him.

The place was steel-walled, steel-ceilinged, steel-floored. Against the bottom wall was the bunk upon which his bedding was heaped. As he sat upon the iron rod forming the edge of this bunk, he had to bend forward so as not to hit with his head the second bunk, above. The upper bunk was without tenant that day. The cell was wide as the length of the bunks—about seven feet—and of less depth. That is, between the bunk and the door, there was just enough room to allow a man to pace the two or three steps allowed by the width; two men could not do it. The door was a steel-barred gate through which the eyes of guards and trusties, watchful or merely hostilely curious, could always peer. In one corner was a three-legged stool; above it, on a triangular shelf, a Bible covered with dust; a placard shone yellow on the wall to the left. That was all.

He sat on the edge of the bunk, his survey made, holding his chin in his two hands, tormented by a strange sensation.

It was an odor; a taint was in the air; something elusive, but which would not go. Curiously enough, in his mind, it called up visions of circus menageries, seen in childhood. After a while he worked out the connection. The smell of a menagerie, it came from caged animals. Here also, there were things in cages. These were not animals; they were men. The taint in the air, it came from men, many men, caged.

The idea made him a little sick. But now, something else was troubling him, something still more vague, more elusive, more irritating than that which he had just caught—something that he must solve.

He felt a vast sense of stoppage—stoppage, that was it. A sense one has on a steamer when suddenly the clanging engines cease with a sigh; that which comes when one is alone in a room with the ticking of a clock, and this ticking stops; the feeling that comes when one passes without warning from the tumult of a storm into a great calm.

There had come a distinct halt in his life; a period, a gigantic punctuation.

9009 was a bad man. He had come to this cell not through a miscarriage of justice. He had been bad; he had been lawless.

He had been lawless from childhood, from the time when, a mere boy, cutting away from a squalid home, he had forced his way to the leadership of a "gang" whose serious occupations were pilfering from the grocer, robbing boats and box-cars, and whose amusements were fierce fights with rival "gangs," stonings of Chinamen, torturings of cats, and experiments in men-vices.

Always he had been at war. He had been at war with men, with society. And now, in this abrupt cessation of the whirl of his life, there had come to him a feeling, vague, indefinite, of futility—a discouragement. All of his fighting, all of his defiance, his cunning had after all led him only to this—a cell. For the last six years he should have been expecting this. But

ch. ends p. 20

really, he had not expected it. It had come to him as a distinct shock. And now came this feeling of uselessness, of futility.

He had fought society and had been worsted. And he felt that always he would be worsted. He felt that he could not go on in this way. It didn't pay, that was it. Always, he would get the worst of it. It didn't pay. He couldn't fight the world. He couldn't fight that. His life—it had been a failure. That was it: his life had been a failure.

It had been a failure. And in him, now, obscure but strong, there was a longing for something else, for some elusive thing that he could not name, that he could not picture, and yet which was indispensable to him.

Strangely enough, it was allied in some way with the impression that he had carried away from his visit to Tom Ryan.

A few weeks before his arrest, Ryan, meeting him on the street, had taken him to his home for dinner. Ryan was one of the companions of his boyhood, and he had not seen him for years.

Ryan had become, he found, a common plodding work-ingman—of the class at which he sneered. He was a hod-carrier.[1] He lived in a wretched cottage on the outskirts of the city. He arrived there every evening, his brogans[2] red with brick dust, his shoulders white with plaster, to squat at a table roughly laden by his wife, and shovel food into his harassed body. That evening Collins had eaten with him.

They sat at the table, Ryan with both elbows upon it, gulping the food which Collins hardly touched. Mrs. Ryan, a squarely built, red-faced woman, stood between the stove and the table, keeping the latter plenished. At intervals she leaned over and directed a wandering spoon into the gaping mouth of Myrtle, the little tow-headed elder daughter, or

[1] A hod is a trough used for transporting loads, usually bricks or mortar, and carried over the shoulder.

[2] Heavy laced, ankle-high work boots made of coarse leather.

leaned over a crib in the corner of the kitchen, lifting a blanket to quiet an acid wail.

After eating, Ryan had lit his pipe, had puffed a while, and then had gone to sleep, there in his chair.

This, to Collins, used to an alert, vigilant existence; to the excitement of long-plotted and carefully executed thefts and of their resultant pursuits; to intervals of Tenderloin luxury,[3] was just the sort of life to be most despised. To him, his lawlessness and cheap luxuries were what elegance is to the rich, beauty to the artist. Like the rich man, like the artist, he naturally revolted at the commonplace of such an existence as Ryan's.

And yet, that night, he had carried with him a vague and inexplicable desire which was still with him now, which in some way was allied with the feeling that had come to him this morning, here, in his cell; which had to do with the discouragement, the sense of failure, the disgust, almost, that tormented him as he looked back along the days that he had lived.

And as he sat here, his fists against his temples, the two things suddenly leaped together, coalesced.

What he desired was that which Ryan had.

What he, 9009, longed for, what his life had failed to give him, what his life must now give him, it was what Ryan had.

It was Security.

"He felt safe," he said to himself with heavy finality.

Then: "Didn't have to look out for no 'bulls.'"

"Didn't have to look out for stool-pigeons."

"Didn't carry no gun."

"He felt *safe*."

He knew now what he wanted, wanted more than wine, money, women, cigars, more than the joy of fight, the iron tang of revolt; he wanted peace, he wanted security, he wanted what Ryan had.

---

[3] In this context, an area of a city noted for vice and corruption, so called because police in that area could eat well due to criminal connections and bribery.

ch. ends p. 20

"No more of this," he muttered; "no more. I'll turn square."

"Square"—not out of any ethical renovation, but "square," very simply, because thus only could he get what now he wanted, which was peace.

By a freak of his mind there came now to him the scratching pen of the clerk booking him. The big book leaped before him; he saw the pen traveling. "Five years and three years."

Eight years! Eight years before he could even begin his new life.

And yet—eight years; after all, it was not so long, eight years! He gave a swift look behind. The last eight years—they had not been so long! In eight years he would be thirty-seven. A man had some years left at thirty-seven!

He had risen to his feet in his excitement and was pacing to and fro along the narrow space between bunk and door. At one of his turns his eyes fell upon the placard stuck to the wall. He stopped, his eyes glued themselves upon the cardboard, a flush came to his heavy cheeks.

"My copper!"—it was almost a shout—"My copper"—he slapped his thigh—"By God, I was almost forgetting my copper!"

Before him, yellow on the blue-black wall, the placard shone; its little black characters danced. He read them carefully.

GOOD TIME

Under the Goodwin Act[4] you have already earned time which has been deducted from your sentence. This time has been deducted as follows:

For the First year, two months;

Second year, two months;

Third year, four months;

Fourth year, four months;

[4] The Goodwin Act of 1864 established a credit system for prisoners that reduced sentence terms for good behavior.

Fifth year, and every year thereafter, five months.

This time has already been earned by you. The law has given it to you, and it belongs to you. Only bad behavior on your part will forfeit this time. It is for you to determine whether or no you will keep this time to your credit; and for you alone.

About the margin of the printed rule he saw penciled figures, many of them, where former occupants had made calculations over and over again. He fell to figuring.

"Thirty-two months—two years and eight months"—that was his copper. He tried it again; a third time; the result was the same. He could gain two years and eight months. He subtracted now. Keeping his copper, there would be left for him to serve only five years and four months.

Five years and four months! That would not be so long! He looked back along his life to get a measure. Five years ago, he was turning his first yegg[5] trick. It wasn't so long, five years. In five years he would be only thirty-four.

He sat down to calm himself. "In five years—I wonder where Nell will be," he said. But the thought did not remain with him long. Almost immediately he returned to the more palpitant subject. He remained silent, bent over, thinking, a long time. And then, solemnly, almost with affection, "My copper," he said softly.

He would work for it, he would treasure it, his "good time," his "copper." There were rules in this place; he would keep them. There was work; he would work. He remembered the words of the garroter and of the sheriff; he would keep to himself, he would obey, he would do anything they told him.

"Oh, *I'll* be good," he said aloud, whimsically; "I'll be *good*, all right."

A step sounded outside in the narrow corridor, the door opened with a rasp, and Jennings, the sallow-faced guard, walked in. He laid his hand roughly upon the shoulder of

---

[5] Theft, especially a burglary or safecracking.

ch. ends next p.

9009 and fixed his white-gray eyes upon him in a stony, passionless stare. 9009 returned the gaze, defiantly, as had been always his habit, in a struggle of man and man. The guard scanned him long, silently, with no expression in his stony face, but a sort of invisible and heavy threat rising like a dull blush into his cheeks. The look chilled; 9009 met it. For a full minute neither pair of eyes shifted, neither flickered. Then the guard loosed his grip and pushed the shoulder away from him.

"By God," he said evenly. "You *are* a bad one."

He turned; the steel door shut; a bar fell heavily into a socket outside. 9009 remained seated on the edge of his bunk, holding his chin in his two hands. The exultation of his discovery, of his resolve, had left him; instead, a vague sense of danger was enwrapping him; he shivered slightly. And to his nostrils again, an obsession, there came the taint; the taint that came from men, caged, like wild beasts.

0004

To hold his copper and to keep to himself—the sheriff knew what he was saying when he had coupled these admonitions. 9009 learned this through several months of silent observation.

He learned, during that time, many things about guards and convicts. First, he found that there were two classes of convicts—the ordinary convict and the trusty. He wondered much at the trusties. He saw them all over the prison. A trusty had supervision of the cells in his tier. A trusty superintended the waiters of the dining hall. The druggist to whom one morning 9009 went for quinine[1] was striped. Convicts kept the prison records. Convicts kept the keys of the cell houses. A murderer serving a life sentence had in his charge nearly all the keys inside the wall.

That the prison officials should trust a felon to the point of placing in his hands the power to free all his fellows was a cause of wonder to 9009. He wondered when he found that another stripes-clad man was allowed to go on errands to the neighboring town unattended. And he marveled at the fewness of the guards. Fifty of the fifteen hundred inmates

---

[1] A bitter crystalline alkaloid compound derived from several species of cinchona bark (native chiefly to the Andes in South America), the salts of which were used as a tonic and antimalarial drug.

could have overpowered with ease all the blue-clad guards within sight at one time, were fifty to act in concert.

He watched and wondered, and these were slow months. Without knowing it, he had begun to let his shoulders droop, and he shuffled slightly now when he walked. Amid many of his kind, he moved alone, silently watching. Daily he saw blue-clad guards carrying loaded rifles. He heard each evening heavy bolts fall loudly into sockets. Each morning he woke to the faint taint in the air.

He rose at six to the resounding clang of a gong in the corridor. The rattle of released locks and jerked bolts was followed by the grate of opening doors, and the convicts, flowing out into the corridors, spent fifteen minutes cleaning them and cleaning their cells. For that time, speaking was allowed; and 9009 noted how some of the stripes-clad men slipped, in passing, stealthy words from moveless lips; gathered about the sinks, others gibed each other cruelly; but some, their eyes on the floor always, muttered to themselves without cease. There was fifteen minutes of this, then, at the gong's stroke, the men, suddenly petrified into silence—the silence that was to last through the day—marched out to the dining hall. From now on no speech was allowed. Silently each man stepped out of his cell, and placed his hands upon the shoulders of the man ahead of him, forming the lock-step line. The guard—he was a grizzled blue-eyed fellow who had lived most of his life in prison—unarmed as were all the guards who worked within reach of the convicts, waited till they were in formation, and then unlocked the door at the bottom of the corridor. With a hissing of feet upon the concrete, the line moved smoothly forward, through this door, into a long outer corridor closed by a steel-barred gate from the yard. The guard, striding ahead, took position at this gate, then, when the line had reached him and had halted compressed and orderly before him, he opened it, letting the linked men out into the yard, under the shadow of the walls, with their pacing guards. Usually, though, at this morning hour, the guards were few.

In the dining hall, the striped felon who had charge of the waiters commanded the line by signals, halting it at the door, then signing it to advance until the convicts were at their places at the tables, which extended the room's length. At another signal, the striped men sat down and began to eat silently. At each end of the hall, overhead in a small barred gallery, a guard stood, holding a rifle, watching the dumb eaters.

They rose from their places at a final signal and, re-forming, crawled outside. 9009, now, was a link, a vertebra, in the monstrous thing. He touched two shoulders before him; he felt two hands touching his shoulders behind. The line crept through the upper yard, along a track beaten as if into stone by its eternal passings, to the gates beneath the turret with its long, wicked muzzle of rapid-fire gun. The gates opened, and it filed out into a lane, between fences twenty feet high, made of barbed wire, to the jute-mill.

They worked without speech in the jute-mill, but 9009 saw some of the convicts, passing among the looms on errands, steal words, sliding them through lips that remained motionless in their down-turned faces. He stood before a whirring loom. At the height of his eyes, behind the multitudinous perpendicular lines of the warp, a clacking shuttle fled swiftly from right to left, from left to right, in unceasing flight. Whenever a thread of warp or whoof broke he had to retie it quickly; whenever the shuttle became bare, he dipped his hand into a basket kept filled by another convict and drew a new one, threading it into place. This is all he had to do—tie strings and change shuttles. The machine did everything else. Started by the mill superintendent—an old Scotchman, the only man in the prison that wore no uniform—it whirred on hour after hour, holding his rigid attention, the clacking shuttle fleeing back and forth before his eyes in incessant flight, till the superintendent, pressing a button, brought it finally to rest and freed him from its exactions.

Across the aisle from 9009, at another loom, stood the red-striped convict whom he had seen in the line the day he had entered the prison; and it was the garroter, with whom he had come in, who had charge of keeping the baskets filled with threaded shuttles. When the garroter had been assigned to this work, a scene incomprehensible to 9009 had taken place. The garroter had pleaded against the order; little beads of sweat had welled up on his forehead; he had almost knelt to Jennings, standing there impassive, his light whip in hand. It had taken the latter's threat of solitary confinement to break the man's resistance.

At noon, the striped line crept to the dining hall and after the meal crept back to the jute-mill. At five o'clock it crept to supper, then to the cell-house, and all the time it had been dumb. Locked in their cells now, the convicts were again allowed to speak. Cellmate spoke to cellmate, quietly; friends threw jocular remarks through the bars; and sometimes enemy reviled enemy in words crawling as with vermin. At counting bell they stood up with faces against the bars while a guard passed, scanning them. At nine o'clock the lights went out abruptly, all save two in the corridor. Then whispered murmurings sounded vague through the shadows, and the guard slipped silently along the tier-walks. The sound of heavy breathing succeeded. And 9009, lying on his back in his bunk, calculated the days, added to the days that were gone, subtracted from the days that were left, and his arms, folding themselves in a weary gesture, seemed to hug to his breast his copper.

The routine changed on Sundays. Twice a month the tenants of the cell houses went out into the yard for a few hours' recess; and twice a month, alternating, came chapel.

The chapel was a long bare room with whitewashed walls and a low ceiling supported by yellow posts. One of these posts, near the doors, had stapled into it, a little more than man-height from the ground, a single big iron ring. Just above this ring, the yellow paint was soiled with an oily smudge, spreading fan-wise, in which showed vague imprints of fingers and thumbs; and the floor immediately below was white and smooth, as if from many scrubbings. This post, on weekdays, was the prison's whipping-post.

The convicts might see visitors, on chapel-days, in a space set apart for this, near the office of the captain of the yard. But no one came to see 9009. And he did not care. He was becoming more and more absorbed in the earning of his copper, absorbed like a miser hoarding gold piece by piece. At times he thought of Nell—but without expectation, in a detached manner. His experience led him to expect nothing of her kind. "Probably hooked up with some guy long ago," was the mental remark with which he usually dismissed thought of her.

Lying in his bunk one night, he was startled by a new and disturbing note in the noise of the sleeping prison, now so familiar to him. It was a rasp, a faint scratching, a rubbing of metal upon metal. He listened; after a while he made sure of the sound. It was the purring rasp of a saw rubbing metal, and it came from the cell next to his.

He knew the two in this cell—knew them from watching them as he watched all the others; they were ugly fellows, who always kept to themselves savagely. And now they were sawing the bars! He sat up on his elbow, listening, his heart a-pound with a contagion of excitement.

A voice reached him, a low voice of warning; there was a moving of bodies, a sly creaking of bunks; then along the steel gangway passed a shadowy guard, his rubber shoes at each step giving a little hiss. A silence followed, or, rather, the noise of the sleeping prison, a heavy animal breathing broken by gurglings and uncouth snorings, but conformant and familiar, free from the startling new note.

But the next night, and for many succeeding nights after, 9009 heard it again—the furtive purr of saw upon bar, then

ch. ends next p.

the low murmur of warning, and, along the gangway, the slight hiss of the guard's rubber shoes. And one noon he saw one of his hard-eyed neighbors snatch a piece of meat from the dining table and conceal it within his blouse; he saw him repeat this on the following day. They must be ready for the break, the break that would lead them to freedom—or to death. Listening to the saw that night (its rasp was sharper, vibrant with a new impatience) 9009 suddenly thought of his copper.

He might be blamed for this; he might be punished for having known; he might lose it, his copper.

The idea of betrayal, however, did not even cross his mind. And the next morning, he learned all about the trusties.

As, at cleaning time, he passed the cell from which had come the sound of sawing, he saw inside of it the trusty who was cell-tender. The man—a lean fellow with pale-blue eyes and red hair—was stooping over the lower bunk, his hand underneath the blankets.

And that night the cell was empty, and soon there went around the prison the news that the guards had taken from the bunks in this cell a revolver and provisions, and had found the bars sawed nearly through. A great light had come to 9009.

It was the trusties! *They* guarded the convicts. They, it was, and not the guards, who were the jailers. And the guards need not watch them; they watched each other. They were informers. They obtained their jobs, with the privileges that went with them, by betrayal; and they held them just so long as they did Judas work. He understood now why they had rat eyes.

The whole system lay open before him. It was a system of vast espionage, of stalking, of spying, of treachery, of betrayal. He himself was being constantly watched, watched with malevolent hope that he might stumble. Confidence in any one, of course, was impossible (he laughed as he thought of his former wonder at the absence of concerted breaks). He must stay alone, trust no one, speak to no one, isolate himself. The sheriff had spoken true; "good old boy," he now thought, almost with tenderness.

This new knowledge dictated his conduct when, a few days later, he was given a cellmate (up to this time he had been alone in his cell). Returning from the dining hall after the evening meal, he found a little bent striped man, with spiky white hair, sitting on the edge of his bunk. The little man sprang to his feet as 9009 entered. "That's your bunk, ain't it," he said in a wheezy voice; "mine's the up one, ain't it?"

9009 stared at him, scowling. The little man's face was black with a mixture of dust and oil that clogged the pores; his eyes were inflamed, and the lower lids drooped, showing the red linings.

"You're going to be in this cell?" at last asked 9009.

"They put me here," answered the little man humbly, "My old mate, he's shoe-trusty now."

9009's defiance bristled at the word. Pushing the little man aside, he threw himself on his bunk, his face to the wall. After a time he heard him climb carefully into the upper bunk—then a fit of hacking cough came to his ears.

Several times, during the night, 9009 found himself awake, listening to this dry, hacking sound, and each time he thought of the new problem before him. When morning came, he had his mind made up.

"You sweep, and I make up the bunk," he said harshly to the new cellmate. "Next week, you make up the bunk and I sweep. And"—his voice rose—"I don't talk to you, and you don't talk to me—understand? I don't want to talk, and I don't want to listen, so don't you open your trap—understand?"

"All right," answered the little man, looking scared, and nodding his head meekly.

0005

9009, standing before his loom, watching through the threads the clacking shuttle speed from side to side, felt a yellow patch of light, which all day had been crawling slowly along the cement floor, strike his rough brogans at last. This told of the ending afternoon, and immediately a number sprang in his mind. 1760! In a few more hours, he would have remaining to serve only 1760 days. 1760—if he held his copper.

He had held it for six months, or, more exactly, for 184 days. Each night he added one day to the time that had gone; each night he subtracted one day from the time yet to be served. These calculations had become a mania with him. He would reduce to days his original sentence, then to days his copper, then his original sentence minus his copper, then his original sentence minus his copper minus the days served, and thus, by a laborious and circuitous path, would arrive to his result—the number of days remaining to be served—with a pleasant sense of surprise.

He had kept rigidly to his line of conduct. He had communicated with no man—convict, trusty, or guard. He had spoken only once, to his cellmate.

"What makes your face so black?" he had asked in a sudden access of childish curiosity.

"I work at the emery wheel in the foundry," the little striped man had answered.

"And what makes you cough that way, so dry and hard like?" 9009 had continued.

"It's the emery dust a-cutting away me lungs," said the little man.

"Umph—that's what's the matter with your eyes," said 9009, looking at the drooping lower lids, showing red. Then, remembering, he had returned to his determined silence.

The yellow patch of light detached itself from the feet of 9009 and began to crawl toward the wall to his left; he watched his shuttle speeding with tireless movement from side to side. There were a hundred looms in the room; they stood in rows, with a scant four feet between the rows. The shuttle of each, flashing along its groove from side to side, snapped sharply into place at the end of each oscillation. "Clack-clack-clack," they went. The whir of the wheels and the smooth slide of moving parts united in a silken fabric of sound; above this, rang the clacking chorus, multitudinous, incessant, like the gossiping tongues of many women. 9009 hated it.

At either end of the long, high room, an iron-barred cage hung from the ceiling. In each cage stood a blue-clad guard, holding his rifle loosely, as though waiting to use it. Two other guards walked the floor of the room. 9009 feared these. They went about quietly, armed only with small canes. They reported infractions of rules and misbehavior; upon them depended the standing of every convict. One of them was Jennings, the sallow-faced guard with the white-gray eyes. Occasionally, feeling a presence, 9009 glanced behind him; at such a time it was always Jennings that he saw. The guard's face was heavy, expressionless; in his eyes was no light. Lying in his bunk at night, 9009 would often see these eyes.

Among the machines, bearing a basket filled with threaded shuttles the garroter moved incessantly. Whenever the garroter came near, 9009 would look unconsciously across the aisle at the red-striped convict, who stood there at his machine sullen and motionless, his arms folded, his face turned down toward the lower roller upon which slid the finished cloth.

For six months 9009 had seen the garroter bear his basket of threaded shuttles, back bent, walking silently. Prison pallor had smeared the thug's face with its coat of gray. This had begun the first morning, when, in spite of his pleadings, he had been assigned to this work. 9009 remembered the grayness and the sweat that had come into the face then. These had never left the face. Always when he came to this part of the room, they were there—a grayness, as of death, and little drops of sweat, as of fear.

The red-striped convict never looked up when the garroter came to his loom, bearing the basket of shuttles. He stood with folded arms, his eyes upon the winding cylinder, almost at his feet, and his face was like a mask. It was like a mask of stone. And it expressed patience, a patience stony because infinite, a patience counting upon the future with absolute assurance.

The garroter always approached the loom of the red-striped convict from behind and from the left—though he must go out of his way to do this. His bearing changed then. He tiptoed on the balls of his feet, and his eyes never left the red-striped convict, standing there arms folded, head lowered, with an impenetrable and slanting expression. It was strange, the way the strangler held his eyes on the other. Even when, having reached the loom, he dropped his basket and transferred the shuttles to the empty basket on top of the loom, he did not move his eyes. His eyes remained motionless while his face, his head, his whole body moved about them. When he stooped to his own basket, his face was turned up; when he reached above into the red-striped man's basket, his face was turned down; always, whatever might be the position of his body, his eyes, fixed, were upon the red-striped convict, standing there, motionless and impenetrable.

ch. ends p. 34

Once the garroter, groping for the upper basket, had dropped the shuttle into the loom, tearing the warp. The red-striped convict had rushed toward one of the pillars, to press the button signaling for the stopping of the machinery; and to the brusque movement, the garroter had shrunk back and cried aloud. Jennings had smiled.

The yellow square of sunshine had reached the wall to 9009's left, now, and was beginning to climb it; in a few moments the Scotchman would press the button which stopped the machinery. Then 9009 would march back with his fellows to the dining hall, and he would have passed his one-hundred-and-eighty-fifth day still holding his copper. He saw the garroter approaching with his basket of shuttles. He looked toward the red-striped convict, standing there with folded arms, his eyes downcast upon the loom's lower rollers. Something new, suddenly, had come into the man's face.

It was something impalpable, yet fairly screaming with meaning. It lay behind the mask, far back in the dull eyes. Something couchant[1] there for days had moved; it had gathered itself and crouched, now, quivering. And in the mask had come a new heaviness, a heaviness that was a satisfaction, almost a satiety. But the man still stood motionless, his arms folded upon his breast, his face turned down.

The garroter came toward him; and, as it always did, his walk changed; he bent forward, touching the floor with the balls of his feet only, his eyes upon the red-striped convict. He stopped—and he did not see what was in the other's downcast, averted eyes, the thing crouching in ambush there. He laid down his basket; he grasped a handful of shuttles— and his gray face was turned upward as he bent. Then the red-striped convict turned upon the garroter.

The strangler's eyes widened, and into them came a great horror. Still bowed down, he looked up into the eyes of the

---

[1] Lying down with the head raised.

other; little drops of sweat welled out upon his gray forehead; his bent limbs strove to straighten——

And then the red-striped convict sprang. And as he sprang 9009 saw his right hand go up from his waistband and flash above his head clutching a long heavy knife of gray-brown steel. The garroter was still striving to rise, and as he strove, the red-striped convict was upon him. He was upon him like a boy playing leap-frog. His two hands, with a crunching sound, sank into the garroter's shoulders; his two legs twined themselves about the garroter's thick neck. The knife in the right hand rose, fell, rose again, fell, rose again, fell; it moved up and down like a swift piston; the heavy blade stabbed and stabbed. And 9009 saw the red-striped convict's face. The mask had dissolved; the distended nostrils breathed and the eyes blazed joy as the red-barred arm plunged up and down, accurately, as if working in a groove, and the red-barred knees crushed the thick neck between them.

The guards' rifles bellowed from the cage overhead. They flashed; their crash filled the long, high room. They crashed again—the red-striped convict and the garroter became a still huddle in the midst of a widening pool on the gray concrete floor.

The looms hummed and purred and the hundred shuttles beat their clacking measure. The striped heap stirred, then was still again. The red-striped convict lay on his back, his knees still gripping the garroter's neck. His upturned face now held no stony mask; its lines had distended in an expression of peace, of great satiety.

Beats of rapid footsteps sounded on the concrete. The machinery came to a stop in a big silence. Smoke wreaths were still hovering overhead as from the lips of an idle smoker; the tang of powder reached 9009's nostrils. Suddenly he realized; realized fully and completely what had happened. A heavy hand fell on his shoulder, grasping it like a vise, and whirled him around where he stood. He faced

ch. ends next p.

the sallow guard with the gray-white eyes; and the guard was half-smiling——

"You dog," said Jennings; "what do you mean by letting a man kill another and saying nothing!" His voice was thick, but his lips showed a sort of satisfaction. 9009 felt anger choke him; he threw back his head and looked square into the lightless eyes; his lips parted in a snarl. And then he thought of his copper, and swallowed hard, keeping silent.

"You go to the head of the line tonight," ended Jennings, and turned toward the bodies.

Two guards were tearing the legs of the red-striped convict from the garroter's neck. It took two to do it. Another picked up something from the huddle of bodies. It dripped as he raised it. 9009 looked at it keenly. It was long, and heavy at the back. It was a file, a rasp file, sharpened to an edge and a point. Files, then, could be obtained and made into this.

The guard, holding it at arm's length, carried the weapon away.

0006

As the line emerged from the jute-mill, 9009, who had placed himself at its head, was called out by Jennings and taken to the office of the captain of the yard. It was the same room in the center of which he had stood on his first day, six months before, following the sputtering pen of the smiling clerk as it wrote his history in an entry of five spaces across the lined page of the book. He now sat on a bench by the door, watching and listening.

The four jute-mill guards were all there; three of them talked in an undertone about the captain's flat-topped desk, but Jennings, though in the group, was silent, toying with the file-knife which lay on the desk. 9009 scanned the weapon; it held a fascination to him. He noted its weight. One could hack or stab with it. It would split a skull or sever a rib. And the red-striped convict had been able to get a file and manufacture this thing, and hide it till ready. A man could do many things under the noses of the guards. If he didn't have his copper to look out for.

9009 drew his eyes away from the knife. In a corner of the room, tilted back in his chair, sat the trusty who, six months before, had taken his picture, with that of the garroter, now dead, and that of the murderer, whom he never saw. The man had not changed. His striped garments, tailored almost to dandiness, were carefully pressed; his patent-leather shoes shone; his linen collar was spotless; in his tie was a pearl scarf-pin. And his shiny black hair was parted foppishly in two bangs that descended upon the low and livid forehead.

A door swung open, and the captain entered. The trusty met him at the desk and began speaking.

He spoke in an undertone, deferentially but persuasively. As he bent his head, passing his tongue between his thin lips, his hazel eyes shifted, showing green light. He held a cigar between his long white fingers; now and then he flicked off the ashes nervously.

The blue-clad captain was shaking his head as he listened, and a frown, cutting the narrow space between his shaggy brows, told of worry. He was built on square lines, and his jaw was heavy, but he showed now no decision in his manner. It was the thin-faced trusty who was deciding through the persuasive hiss of his whispering. Fragments of sentences reached 9009. They were discussing the punishment of some convict, some convict other than himself.

"Dangerous man—these two breaks, remember—not broken," in detached hissing bits from the trusty, whose eyes flickered green.

Then the subdued but big growling voice of the captain: "A long talk with him—talked right—willing to be a good dog—two years solitary—broken now."

Again the detached hisses: "Yes, but—remember—bad one—more."

The whispering sunk still lower; an assurance was coming into the trusty's manner. The captain's head dropped in assent. He had evidently yielded. But the perplexed frown was still on his forehead as now he turned to the guards. The trusty followed him. His white face was placid with satisfaction. A hot hate rose through 9009. So that was the way they did it; that was the way they sent a man to the solitary or to the whipping-post! Unconsciously, his eyes roved back to the knife, lying there, heavy, upon the desk.

One after the other, the jute-mill guards told their stories of the murder and of the shooting to the captain while he sat at his desk, listening closely. The trusty sat near him, making notes on a short hand pad, his sharp, white face thrust avidly forward. The captain listened in silence, drumming on the desk with his thick fingers. Once he picked up the file-knife and examined it. Occasionally a guard would halt at a sign from the trusty and would repeat some part of his statement. Each, as he finished, left the office, and finally it was Jennings' turn to speak. He bent his face close to the captain's and talked a long time. 9009 could not catch a word of what he said; but once he saw the captain look up and glance sharply toward him. Then Jennings straightened up. He had finished. He looked into the captain's eyes. The captain nodded silently, a triple nod that told understanding, agreement, and promise. Jennings turned and went out. The case of 9009 had been decided.

Suddenly 9009 found himself on his feet, and a hoarse voice that he hardly recognized as his own was bellowing: "Say, don't I get any say about this? Don't I get any say?"

The trusty, who was near the door, turned and threw back a glance half curious, half ironical, then went on softly, on the balls of his feet, into an inner office. The captain did not look up; he sat drumming the desk with his thick fingers. But the scowl had deepened between his shaggy brows, and his eyes had become very small. 9009 dropped back upon the bench; he gripped the edge and waited. And again, irresistibly, his eyes wandered to the file-knife, lying heavy on the desk.

"Collins, come over here." The captain's voice was quiet, but leaden. 9009 rose slowly and came near, the desk between them. The captain took the file-knife and locked it in a drawer above his knees. Then he sat regarding the convict in silence. As he looked into the somber eyes of the captain and at the scowl between his shaggy brows, 9009 let his head go back, stiffening his thick neck, and his under-jaw thrust itself slightly forward. He could not help it; the movement was a pure reflex, as unconscious as the threat-grimace of a

ch. ends p. 41

dog meeting the growl of another dog. The captain watched the change, searching the hard face before him. Then he spoke, slowly, uttering each word with great distinctness.

"You watched Japanese Tommy kill Thurston this afternoon, and you didn't call a guard nor make a signal." He paused. A twitch of protest rose from 9009's feet along his whole body. But it had not time to find voice; the captain was speaking again, with his heavy pounding inflection: "And a month ago you heard Smith and Boone saw their bars; you heard 'em for weeks—and you said nothing."

9009 sickened. He had the sensation as of a great net which had fallen about him, over his head, around his arms. They had known this all the time! They had known it and had kept it all this time waiting for their good chance. He continued staring at the captain, eye to eye, silently, but a little haze of sweat, like the film on the window-pane of a heated room, was coming upon his forehead.

"Wilson!" the captain called out without moving.

The trusty came from the inner office. His tongue passed between his thin lips, catlike. "Get me number eight key," said the captain.

"I know you like a book," the captain went on, almost indifferently to 9009; "I've handled the likes of you for years, and"—he paused thoughtfully—"I generally manage to break you fellows." He glanced up sharply at 9009 and without looking took a heavy key from Wilson who had come with it behind him; then went on, pointing at the key with his index finger. "You come here thinkin' you were bigger than the guards; and we've known you from the start, and watched you. You're the kind that generally manage to lose your copper"—9009 went yellow. The captain rose and stood still a moment. "You *ought* to lose it for this affair," he went on—9009 swallowed hard—"but I'm going to give you one more chance; I'll give you a taste of what we have for you bad men." He weighed upon the last three words heavily, with ponderous sarcasm, but this was lost on 9009. He was taking a big gulp of relief. "Come on," said the captain.

They went, without a word, across the yard, to one of the cell-houses, and down a flight of stairs, to the basement. The captain stopped before a heavy door of oak, studded with spikes, and signed to a trusty who met him there. The man swung open the outer door of oak, and then an inner door of smooth steel. 9009 entered. The door creaked shut behind him; the outer door slammed; he heard a bolt fall. And there was no longer sound or sight.

He stood on a steel floor, in darkness. This darkness was absolute. It seemed to have weight, to press down upon him. It smothered. And there was no sound. It was as though he were buried deeply with tons and tons of silent earth upon him. He stood still a long moment, while this feeling enwrapped him slowly; then he stepped forward on tiptoe, reaching with hands before him, till he touched a wall. It was of steel, and he ran his fingers over rivets. Face to this wall, he moved to the right, struck a corner, then another wall; another corner, another wall; another corner; another wall; a fourth corner, and the wall from which he had started. But missing his tale,[1] he went about a fifth corner, counting it as the fourth, felt a vague sense of mistake, and then, suddenly, a dizziness made him sway on his legs. He had lost his bearings; it was as if, about a pivot upon which he stood, the whole world had revolved several times.

Controlling the sickness within him, he went around the cell several times, eyes shut, groping carefully; and at last, like a blessing, there came to his fingertips the feel of the joining of the door-edge; and the world, swinging, readjusted itself; and again, in his head, like a reassurance, he held the plan of the prison. Preserving this carefully, he dropped to his hands and knees and crawled over the floor. It stretched, smooth, without a wrinkle, between the four smooth walls; there was on it nothing, not a stool, not a blanket—nothing.

---

[1] In this context, a number counted off.

ch. ends next p.

He stood up in the center. There oozed to him not a drop of light; above his head, cold eddies of air passed like vague beings. A desire was growing within him—a desire to beat upon the floor and walls, to hammer and to shout.

To resist it, he sat upon the floor; it was cold and very hard. He tried to lie down and relax himself to patience. He began to wonder how long he had been here. He did not know if it was an hour or a minute.

He tried talking to himself. A timidity, a diffidence[2] overwhelmed him as he heard this voice, sounding strange to him. He closed his lips. But in a little while he heard himself again speaking aloud, and he was cursing. According to the legends of prison life, this is a sign of coming insanity; so, crouching in the center of the walled-in darkness, he occupied his mind by counting his copper.

He reduced to days his sentence; then to days his copper; then to days his sentence minus his copper; then to days his sentence minus his copper minus the days already served. He did this many times, by different processes.

But insensibly he passed from this, and a vision came to him. As he crouched here in the center of this cubical compressed blackness, he saw suddenly the captain's flat-topped desk, and the knife upon it. He saw this sharply—its gray color, spotted with brown stain, its heavy back, with the file-rasp still upon it, the keen blade, the needle-like point; he could feel its weight, its well-balanced weight, that admitted of cracking a skull or carving out a rib.

Then he saw the red-striped convict spring upon the garroter leap-frog fashion and entwine his legs about his neck while the knife went up and down with a pumping movement. He saw his nostrils, breathing joy as he stabbed, stabbed again, stabbed, stabbed; his eyes blazing joy. And he saw him lying on his back, his legs still entwined, looking up with his white face, now full of peace and of satiety——

When, the next morning after breakfast, the captain of

[2] Lack of self-confidence; timid or shy.

the yard saw 9009 emerge from the dungeon, he noted that the convict's eyes were bloodshot, and that heavy lines had sprung, overnight, from the ends of the nostrils to the corners of the mouth.

0007

"LISTEN!" A shock-headed, square-bodied little safecracker, called "Shorty" Hayes, and doing fifty years, admonished 9009 in the subtle language of those who are watched.

The two sat on a board, suspended by ropes from the roof, far above the ground, painting the wall. They had been working all day and had arrived to the space immediately below the windows of the office of the captain of the yard.

"Shorty" did not speak aloud. He did not use his tongue at all. He talked with his eyes—a single sharp shifting of the eyeballs and a flash of light from them, both shift and light-flash moving toward the window, slightly ajar just above their heads.

It was Jennings who was talking within the office. His voice, suddenly, had gone to a lower key. "Things are moving," he said quietly.

There was the creak of an office-chair turning in its socket; then the subdued but big growling voice of the captain.

"Good. Will it come through?"

The voice of Jennings came back with metallic positiveness.

"Yes—four of them are framing. Inside of a month that fool Miller will be giving away his clothes again and telling his friends he's going to be paroled. There'll be a dozen of them in it by that time——"

"Can we handle it?" The captain's voice was anxious.

"Leave that to me. One of the four is my man. How's the warden?"

"The governor is just aching for a chance to get at him. You work that, and he's done for. And there'll be something for you and me——"

Just then, the trusty in charge called 9009 and the safe-cracker down for dinner, and 9009 heard nothing more. He was not interested, anyway. He was still keeping to himself with savage determination and hugging his copper. In that alone was he interested, in that and a subtle combat which was going on between himself and the whole prison.

He had become—he saw this plainly—the butt of a series of petty persecutions which he ascribed to Jennings. This painting was one of them. The turpentine made him deathly sick, yet he was kept at it for a straight three weeks. He was often given the more loathsome prison work. At meals, if a convict within ten places from him broke the rule by talking, it was he, 9009, who was accused and punished by being deprived of his next meal. At the jute-mill Jennings tormented him subtly. He would plant himself behind 9009, boring into his back with his hard eyes, while the convict fought, under these conditions, to keep his attention rigid upon the machine, with its ceaseless exactions.

What had happened was this. From the first Jennings had decided that 9009 was a "bad one." He had sowed this belief into the mind of the captain of the yard. The captain had passed it on to the other guards. And the trusties had soon caught the hint. Jennings, the captain, and the guards were engaged in "breaking" 9009; the trusties, catching with their infallible noses the desire of their protectors, were cease-lessly watching for 9009's first stumble, counting up already the Judas reward that would come of it. But 9009 did not understand all this. He knew only, vaguely, that he was being attacked, and that he must not strike back.

Of these persecutions, depriving him of his sunlight was the worst.

Every alternating Sunday, the inmates of one of the cell-houses had two hours of recreation in the yard while those of the second cell-house were at chapel.

For two of these alternating Sundays it had rained. When the third came, 9009 was famished. It was sunny in the yard; a soft breeze, laden with a scent of warm, wet earth and lush grass was rolling languidly over the walls; it passed the chapel and carried to the cell-house the sound of women's voices, singing. But the men in the cell-house did not listen. They stood at lock-step in the corridor, their feet shuffling on the concrete floor. The line was moving very slowly toward the outer door; at times a tremor as of impatience passed along its gray links.

Jennings stood at the door of the cell-house. As each man slid forward to him, he handed him a slip of paper—his pass. Without this pass, no convict could stay in the yard. The sallow guard glanced coldly at each felon; occasionally his white-gray eyes roved back along the line. Once, as they settled upon 9009, they glinted; then the blurring film crept back over them.

Finally 9009, now the head of the diminished line, was standing at the door, his eyes upon the ground, his right hand held up for the pass, and there was a weary hunger in his face.

"Well?" said Jennings sharply.

"My pass," said 9009, his eyes on the ground, his hand still held out.

"Go on," said Jennings; "don't be stopping the line."

"My pass," repeated 9009 doggedly; "you didn't give me no pass."

"You lie," said Jennings evenly; "how many passes do you want?"

9009's hand dropped; then rose again in mute begging gesture.

"Move on," Jennings ordered.

The striped line surged forward, and 9009, forced through the door, passed out into the sunlit yard.

ch. ends p. 49

It was warm; the sunshine was a golden downpour; the breeze, rolling languidly over the wall, fell into the yard heavy with the scent of wet earth and lush grass; a bee, afloat upon it, came buzzing from the outer world and thrice circled 9009 with its murmur, like a consolatory secret. And the earth, hard-beaten though it was by thousands of clumsy brogans, was springy under foot, elastic as steel and concrete were not; and the dome above was high and blue, and away up at its apex was a little white cloud. When you looked up at the little white cloud, it seemed to recede, farther and farther up and away; but when, after deceiving it by gazing at the ground for a time, you looked up at it again, there it was, back in the same place. Vaguely 9009 enjoyed all this; but all the time he was moving from group to group, trying to evade as long as possible the guard who had begun already to collect the passes.

There was noise in the yard, the noise of men's voices lifted unrestrained, like the voices of boys in a schoolyard. The convicts had thrown themselves into play with violence.

Two sides were busy in a ball game. A ring of stripes-clad spectators pressed close about the home-plate where "Shorty," the shock-headed, square-bodied little safecracker, was standing, swinging his bat in circles, bringing it down upon the plate resoundingly. He was jeering the pitcher, a long pale-faced sneak-thief who, winding himself up ostentatiously for his delivery, looked in his stripes like a snake upright on its tail. And behind this one and to the right, a short wiry pickpocket bent his body and straightened it nervously, and rubbed his thin-fingered hands together, watching the batter with ferret eyes. Behind the safecracker, a tall, gaunt highwayman[1] named Miller—he had been leader in several attempts to escape and had a mania for giving away his clothes before such breaks—crouched in his red stripes, eyes gleaming. Suddenly the pitcher's contorted body unlocked with a snap; the ball sped, white in

---

[1] One who robs on public roads.

the sunlight; the safecracker swung his bat with terrific force, wildly; the ball thumped into the broad mitt of the red-striped highwayman. "Strike one," yelled the umpire, a stony-faced confidence-man. The crowd whooped. The safecracker spat in his hands, taking his bat with a new grip. The pickpocket threw a back handspring.

In a corner, near the stone building where were the condemned and solitary cells, two bullet-headed burglars were shoving their hands into tattered boxing gloves; without premonitory fiddling, they began slamming blows thick and fast into each other's faces. Near them, men were pitching quoits,[2] using horseshoes; they capered wildly as the horseshoes rose high into the air, and shouted after them as if to direct their flights.

All these men played without repression, with violence. And even those who merely walked, singly or in pairs, threw out their legs like horses just out of the stable. All save a few who paced stiffly with bowed heads, hands folded behind them—they were old-timers—and one or two who stood still or moved only to spasms of impulse, talking aloud to themselves—these had tempted madness by counting their days too often in the darkness of dungeon or drear of "solitary."

"Where's your pass?"

9009 started. He had forgotten, watching the others.

"I got none," he said sullenly to the guard at his elbow.

"Go in, then."

The guard spoke without passion or resentment, almost wearily. He waved his hand toward the cell-house. 9009 went back to his cell.

He went back to his cell and sat down on his three-legged stool. After a while, still seated, he began to slide the stool across the steel floor in little jumps, his eyes, meanwhile, turned upward attentively. When thus, in small tentative slides, he had covered the few square yards of the cell's free

---

[2] A game in which players toss rings of metal, rope, or rubber at an upright peg or stake in the hope of encircling or landing as near as possible to it.

ch. ends next p.

area, he returned to a point near the center, moved a fraction of an inch forward, then a still smaller fraction to the right, and was still, his big clasped hands hanging loosely between his knees, his face turned upward. The posture emphasized the heaviness of his jaw, the ugly lines from ends of nostrils to corners of mouth; but even then, it was an attitude almost of prayer.

He was gazing, past the bars, on and up through a little window near the ceiling of the cell-house, at a patch of sky. It was a little patch, irregularly framed by the top and right side of his cell-door and the sill and left side of the window, and slashed angularly by the roof of a near building; and exactly where he sat it showed a bit larger than it did from any other place in the cell. It was blue, a very tender blue; when 9009 stared at it hard, the faint taint in the air of the cell-house, with its added Sunday reek of chloride of lime, left him, and he seemed to breathe again that heavy, warm and sweet air which was rolling over the wall, into the prison yard. He sat on the stool, back bent (with his head low he could see more of the blue), his hands hanging between his knees, his face turned upward; gradually his lips loosened, his heavy jaw dropped, and in his eyes, looking up in that attitude, almost of prayer, there came slowly an expression of longing, of vague patient longing, like a dog's.

It was very still in the cell-house. At times, as if from far off, there came the attenuated tumult of the yard; in the air was the taint, and the added Sunday reek of chloride of lime. But 9009 was unconscious of this. He looked. Bowed on his seat, he looked up with loose lips and troubled eyes at the little patch of blue sky. After a while a film seemed to creep into it. Gradually this deepened into a whitish opalescence. It was a cloud; 9009 fancied it was the cloud that he had seen earlier in the day, when in the yard. He cast his eyes down to play with it again, to play the receding and approaching game of hide-and-go-seek. When he looked up again, the cloud was gone. It had been a very little cloud. And the blue was again there, the fresh tender blue.

A step sounded along the corridor; a shadow cut off the light; 9009 dropped his eyes levelly across the bars. Jennings was standing there, looking at him.

He looked at 9009 curiously, a long moment, then looked up at the window, far above. He glanced back into the cell, then, turning his back, shifted his position a foot. The patch of blue disappeared.

9009 remained where he was; his lips were no longer loose, his jaw did not droop, and the expression in his eyes was not of longing. The guard stood there, motionless; his back, square and brutal, rose like a wall before the cell-door.

For a long time they were thus. Occasionally, from the yard outside, there came whoops, cries of animal enjoyment; and again in the air was the taint, the taint from many cages nearby. The afternoon waned, dusk came, the convicts returned; and then Jennings spoke.

"I'm going to break you," he said; then turned on his heel and strode off down the corridor.

On the next Sunday, 9009 was again denied his pass, and the window, which had been white washed during the week, was closed, cutting off the patch of blue. After that, 9009 ceased to ask for his pass; he spent his Sunday afternoons on his back, staring up at the bunk above him.

Sometimes his cellmate, the little black-faced, spike-haired man, returning from the yard turned upon him his inflamed eyes with a strange look, almost of wistfulness, as though he wanted to speak; but 9009 mastered a desire to break their silence, and lay without a word, staring upward sullenly.

0008

9009 gripped two bars of his cell-door and shook the steel till the rattle went resounding down the corridor in harsh crescendo.

"Here—you up there in 17, be quiet or I'll throw you into the dungeon!"

The voice of the night guard came up through the shadows; it had the tone of one who is irritated by a common annoyance. 9009 stepped back quickly and threw himself on his bunk. "What's got into me, anyhow?" he whispered up to his cellmate, in the bunk above him.

They had arrived by this time to a certain degree of confidence. This had begun one day when, as 9009 was returning, grim and sullen, from his third short term in the dungeon, the little black-faced, spike-haired man had drawn from his blouse two pieces of bread that he had stolen from the dining room and had handed them to him without a word.

"What's got into me," whispered 9009; "am I going nuts?"

"I used to get that way," wheezed back the little man from the darkness above; "lots does it; it's spells comes on you."

9009 stretched himself out flatly and took hold of the sides of his bunk. He was afraid. He had caught himself at this sort of thing before; he feared this new impulse which crouched within him now always, hiding stealthily for days to spring out without warning and contort his sinews to action. Two or three times it had roused within him suddenly as, marching in the lock-step line, he stole a look up at the guard on the wall, pacing with his gun loose in hand, like a hunter; it had bidden him rush for the wall. Twice in the jute-mill, with Jennings behind him, it had told him to turn upon the sallow guard—and so loudly, so commandingly had it ordered, that he had almost obeyed before taking other thought. And this time, when at the sound of the guard's voice he had found himself with hands knotted about his bars, he knew that again the thing had taken possession of him, convulsing his being.

It came always strongest after a period of strange half-delirious insomnia, during which his mind left him and wandered through the world outside the walls. These periods came often, and lasted sometimes as long as a week. Every night, then, leaving his body tossing, hot, on the narrow bunk in the steel cell, his mind, leaping the walls, flitted from place to place in the wide open world. Dawn saw him always haggard after one of these nights of semi-freedom, and within him the impulse would be crouching, stealthy, waiting to trap him to action. He watched against it incessantly, but a huge irritation vibrated along his nerves.

The whole atmosphere about him, anyhow, now held a suppressed excitement. He had felt it at first as an indefinable thing, a vague restlessness. Then he had become conscious of a subtle change in the routine about him. After several days of close observation, he had been able to place this.

Every morning, now, at cleaning time, as striped men with brooms and creaking buckets passed along the corridors or massed by the sinks, gibing cruelly or sliding lipless words from dead faces, four convicts would gather, heads close together, for a few moments. Each morning the same four, in the same apparently accidental manner, came together near the sinks and conferred for a few moments, saying little, and most of that with their lid-hidden eyes, swiftly.

9009 had marked these four men. One was Miller, the

red-striped highwayman who was catching in the ball game the day that 9009 had been denied his pass. He was a big, gaunt man with a neck made crooked by a gunshot scar; he had made several attempts at escape in the past, and had a mania for giving away his clothes before each of such breaks. The second man was the ferret-eyed, wiry pickpocket who had played shortstop; the third was one of the bullet-headed burglars who had been boxing, and the fourth was Nichols, the stony-faced confidence-man who had umpired the game.

When these four talked, their speech was different from that of the others. It held purpose. When no guard was near, it was tense and hurried; and when guard, trusty, or ordinary convict approached, it sprang up into spasms of argument or rough laughter. The arguments were too vibrant and the laughter was too loud. In these stolen conferences Nichols, the stony-faced confidence-man, seemed to be leader.

"Here, you up in 17; try that again and I chuck you into the dungeon!"

The voice of the guard came up through the shadow, and 9009 again found himself with hands knotted about bars, while down the corridor came still the echo of rattling steel.

He threw himself back upon his bunk, and stretched himself flat, taking hold of the rods at the sides. "Pard," he whispered, "I *am* going nuts."

"It's just spells," came back the pacifying wheeze from above; "just spells; we all have 'em."

9009 lay on his back, motionless, staring up into the darkness. Above him, at regular intervals, drearily, there sounded a dry weary coughing.

"What makes ye cough—so so hard and dry-like," he asked at length. He had asked this several times before, and knew; but now, suddenly, he wanted to talk.

"'Tis the emery dust a-cuttin away me lungs," the answer returned from the darkness.

"It's worse every day," went on 9009.

ch. ends p. 58

There was a silence; then words floated down again. "It keeps ye awake nights?" said the invisible cellmate meekly.

"I guess. Yes——" 9009 kicked at his blanket viciously.

They were quiet for a time. A guard hissed by in his rubber shoes along the gangway.

"You ought to kick," 9009 began again. "I'd roar till somebody heard."

Two words fell back through the darkness. "No use."

"Why in hell don't you go to the hospital?"

"Can't."

They were silent for a long time. The darkness lay upon them like a heavy vapor, lay upon the strong man in the lower bunk, tortured with twitching nerves, upon the little man above, nauseated with weakness; it lay upon them heavy, tainted, without mercy, turned from the sweet poppy-consoler to a hostile, sullen power keeping them awake to their torments. And the little man began to cough, a long dreary fit that seemed to have no end.

When it did terminate, 9009 let out a big breath; he found that he had held it all through the time that his mate was coughing. He lay silent a while longer, then, hesitatingly, "C'n I—help you—anyways?" he asked.

The response was slow in coming; then it dropped down softly. "Ye're the first man as ever asked me that in this hell-hole," said the little cellmate.

They were quiet again, long. 9009 had thrown off his blanket and lay very still. But the darkness now was less heavy upon him; between the two bunks it seemed to have become less opaque, to have parted a bit to let through a softness.

"Ye can't help me," began the voice above again; "ye can't; nobody can't. I'm up against the push. It's this way:

"I left this hell-hole once, left it on parole, and I got throwed back. I got throwed back. Fer why? Fer why did I get throwed back? What do ye think? Fer stealin'? Fer killin'?

Fer snuffing a gofe?[1] Fer cookin' a bull? Guess why. Fer why did I get throwed back?"

The voice had risen clear now, pitched thin like a penny whistle; the questions dropped upon 9009 fiercely insistent. He lay silent, waiting, and at length the questioner, whom he could feel leaning out of his bunk above him, answered himself:

"I got throwed back in this hell-hole," he said, "fer marrying. Yes," he repeated drearily; "fer marrying.

"Ye see, I was doing ten years"—the words, long repressed, now came flowing one upon the other tumultuously—"I was doing my ten spot and had five done already; and I got hold of religion. Oh, 'twas on the square all right. I know now it's all rot, but I was on the square then. I was psalm-singing, and they got me paroled——

"It's a fine thing, that parole business. If ye've got a bad friend in the world, he's got ye. Every man has ye foul. Did you ever read the rules for paroled cons? Ye can't breathe the wrong way, or back ye go. Ye're a con just the same. And the whole outside is yer prison. And every citizen is a stool-pigeon a-watching to tell on ye.

"Well, I'd made bad friends in the pen. Wan was yer friend Jennings (9009, in the darkness below, exploded in an oath); t'other was that cat-faced trusty of the captain's office, Wilson (9009 swore again and spit out of his bunk). The two was just starting the dope ring—selling opium to the cons. I was a trusty, a-tending the cells. They needed the cell-tenders to peddle the dope to the cons, an they thought I was just the man fer that because I was playing smooth in the chapel. But I was on the square about that chapel business. I wouldn't stand fer their graft. And so they tried to job me, but my friends on the outside who'd got me religion, they beat them to it and got me paroled.

"Well, I learned all about that parole snap in short order. The first month I was in the city I got pinched six times

---

[1] Gofer.

ch. ends p. 58

by the perlice fer jobs I didn't know nothing about. Every time a bull or detective passed me, he pinched me fer luck; and between them and their stool-pigeons I was ready to jump out of the State. But then I got to the Whosoever Will Mission where they take in ex-cons. They treated me good, and I lived wit them. And then——

"I met a girl there."

9009 thought of Nell, and swiftly, as usual, he put the thought from him.

"I met a girl there. She'd been on the town and turned straight. Ye know that kind; if they turn square, and it's on the square wit them, they're so straight all hell couldn't touch them. Well, that was her. A slip of a girl, and she was nursing and working in the mission. They had a sort of hospital for broken-down bums, and she was taking care of them old whiskey-soaks. Well, we got stuck, and we didn't give a cuss for them parole rules, and the mission people, they thought it'd be all right, and we got married——

"A con can't get married, and a con on parole is a con. Jennings, he came down to the city on his vacation and seen the marriage license in the paper. We'd been married wan day when they pinched me.

"They throwed me back here and put me in the foundry at the emery wheel, and the emery wheel is a-cuttin' away me lungs. Jennings, he fixes the jobs; he's a-gettin' back at me."

The voice in the darkness above stopped. A long dreary fit of coughing followed. 9009, lying on his back, straining his eyes upward, thought of Nell, and put the thought out of his mind. "What's become of her," he asked curiously; "of the girl you got stuck on and married?"

"Oh," came back the cellmate's voice, and all the shrill strength was out of it, and it fell down heavy as lead; "Oh, she's cut out religion—gone back to hell!"

They sank into a final silence; again the darkness drew about them, crushing, tainted, without mercy. Above, the little man coughed, drearily, endlessly; below, the strong man twitched to the torture of his nerves; and to their ears, uncouth and fantastic, there came the breathing of the prison.

And after a while, like a kindness, sleep enwrapped the upper bunk. And in the lower, 9009 felt slowly his mind leave his tossing body to wander over walls, in the free wide world. He lay there, in semi-ecstatic insomnia; his senses were drugged. Suddenly they awoke to a tapping.

They awoke and were immediately alert. From a cell down the corridor, there came a tapping, a soft tapping, faint but insistent:

"Tap-tap (pause); tap-tap (long pause); tap-tap-tap-tap-tap (pause); tap (long pause); tap-tap-tap (pause); tap-tap-tap-tap (long pause); tap-tap"—it stopped.

And immediately, from another cell, alert, tense, and affirmative: "Tap-tap; tap-tap; tap-tap."

Then, again from the first cell, very softly, but with insistence, the first call: "tap-tap (pause); tap-tap (long pause); tap-tap-tap-tap-tap (pause); tap (long pause); tap-tap-tap (pause); tap-tap-tap (long pause); tap-tap."

And from far down the corridor, a third cell spoke; decisively, almost ragefully: "tap-tap; tap-tap; tap-tap."

"Tap-tap," began the first cell again; "tap-tap; tap-tap-tap-tap-tap"——

It broke off short; to 9009 came again the prison's uncouth breathing; then, shadowy, a guard passed along the cells, hissing in his rubber shoes.

The tapping was not resumed. It was some alphabetical communication, 9009 knew; he had heard of such a thing. Lying on his back he thought of the four men—of Miller, the gaunt highwayman, of the pickpocket, the bullet-headed burglar, the stony-faced confidence-man—who met every morning by the sinks and talked lipless words; and after a while he felt himself sinking into a blessed somnolence.[2]

"Here, you up there in 17; stop it, stop it!"

And again 9009 awoke to find himself up against his

---

[2] Sleepiness; drowsiness.

ch. ends next p.

cell-door, his hands knotted about the vibrating bars; and from the depths of the corridor there came to him the harsh echo of rattling steel.

This time the little window near the roof was pale with dawn.

0009

At the crash of the morning gong, 9009, haggard with the night, stepped out of his cell, now unlocked for him. One by one the other cells were opening, and the convicts were pouring out upon the gangway, holding brooms and creaking buckets. As he stood by the sinks, 9009 watched the convicts narrowly; but this morning, Miller, the pickpocket, the burglar, and Nichols, the confidence-man, did not meet as usual. They remained apart, each doing his work at a different time.

But when, to the second clang of the gong, 9009 stood with his mate in front of his cell to take his place in the line, now silently forming for its march to the dining hall, he felt suddenly his heart leap up into his throat. A few places ahead of him were Miller, the pickpocket, the burglar, and the confidence-man. They did not belong there, and they did not belong together. Each convict was supposed to take his place in line by standing in front of his own cell; their proper places were somewhere near the middle of the line, and apart from each other. But here they now stood before 9009, close to the head of the line, and together—Miller, the pickpocket, the burglar, and Nichols, in this order. And their heads were bowed toward the floor in involuntary attitudes of deprecation; and from their faces oozed a slanting expression that recalled to 9009 the red-striped convict of the jute-mill waiting at his loom for the garroter.

The guard in charge—a grizzled old blue-eyed fellow who had lived most of his life in prison—wearily saw the line formed, then shuffling on his rheumatic legs to the door at the foot of the corridor, he opened it, and the line began to flow slowly through it into the outer corridor. Leaning against the wall, he let it crawl by till its head was halfway down the long, narrow way, then walked on along its side, briskly, to intercept it at the second door, a steel-barred gate. There he would stand till the line was well massed, and then, unlocking, would let it crawl out into the yard, beneath the shadow of the wall. 9009 watched him as he went along the line with forced briskness, upon legs dragging a bit with the prison rheumatism.

But he never reached the door. Passing along the line, he stopped suddenly with a swift look of surprise; he had noted Miller, the pickpocket, the burglar, and the confidence-man together there near the head, out of their places. The look of surprise flowed instantly into one of suspicion—then his blue eyes gleamed bravely as he turned, at bay. Red-striped Miller had rushed upon him.

The lank highwayman's arms shot out, and his fingers, working, clutched for the guard's throat; but the old man, stepping back toward the wall, struck as he came, full and fair upon the snarling mouth. For a flash the guard was clear; then the pickpocket glided out of the line.

The lithe little felon was half-doubled, his ferret face a-twitch with fierce excitement; he swerved to the left, past Miller, and around the side of the guard as the latter struck out for the second time. He threw out his right arm and at the same time raised his right knee. The arm whipped around the guard's neck like a snake; the knee thumped against the small of the guard's back. The gray head snapped backward, the eyes bulging; for the fraction of a second the body arched itself, still up, then broke and slapped the floor.

Two trusties were coming on the run; the burglar, still in line, pivoted like a mad top on one heel, his right leg held out horizontally; there was a sickening thud, and the first trusty crumpled with a gasping hiccough.[1] The burglar's right hand went to his trouser band, then flashed up—and the second trusty threw himself face down upon the floor. A gasp went through the petrified line; the burglar held in his right hand a heavy black revolver. Miller's hand went to his waist band in a swift fumble; it rose; it also held a heavy black revolver. Then the line dissolved in a chaos of fleeing convicts.

They avalanched past 9009 with pounding feet, as he stood, rooted, on the threshold of the door between the two corridors; and glancing over his shoulder he saw them pop into their cells like rabbits into their holes. But three of the convicts, besides Miller, the pickpocket, the burglar, and the confidence-man had stayed; and now these three, like wild beasts, were hurling themselves against the bars of the outer gate. Miller sprang upon the guard, lying on the concrete floor, still entwined by the pickpocket. He raised his heavy revolver and he struck the gray head once, twice, thrice—and stupidly 9009 noted that the blows thudded not as the revolver fell, but as it rose. A red patch, as if oozing out of the pores, masked the guard's face slowly. The pick-pocket, twitching as a fox-terrier above a squirrel hole, was fumbling madly about the limp blue heap. Suddenly his hand rose, triumphant, holding a great steel key. He leaped to his feet and, bent low, slid like a streak of fire to the outer door. Miller followed him. The burglar remained over the two prostrate trusties, swinging his revolver from side to side. The confidence-man, tiptoeing backward, was coming slowly toward 9009.

He was crouching in the doorway between the two corridors, face forward, his sinews aching with the contagion of action; but his big knotted hands were pressed hard, white-knuckled, upon the sides of the doorway, and "the copper, the copper," he was murmuring. A shout came to him from behind. He threw a glance over his shoulder; he

---

[1] Hiccup.

ch. ends next p.

had a fleeting glimpse of his cellmate's black face peering at him out of his cell with a shocked expression; and, further down, Shorty Hayes, the shock-headed little safecracker, was also looking at him out of his cell, his face all a-gape with a queer sneering laughter. His eyes plunged ahead again, into the outer corridor. Nichols was slowly nearing him, still walking backward, on tiptoe. Suddenly his hand rose; a shot cracked close; a hot spark of powder stung 9009's cheek; the burglar seemed to sink out of sight—and the con-fidence-man, bending, passed beneath 9009's outstretched arms and ran into the inner corridor, holding a weapon that smoked. Through the slight haze 9009 still peered forward. He could see the burglar again now, sprawled upon the floor, kicking his striped legs grotesquely. The three convicts had ceased tearing at the gate; they were crouching now at the foot of its bars, all a-twitch, while Miller and the pickpocket bent at the lock, muttering horrible curses. The red-striped highwayman glanced over his shoulder; his lips drawn back, showed a row of long, yellow teeth. A clang of working lock resounded. The three at the foot of the bars writhed in an agony of impatience. 9009, without knowing it, was moving down the corridor now, stalking, bent low, slowly, step by step, and his outspread hands slid along the walls at either side.

A hard little paw fell upon his left hand; a voice sounded in his ear: "Come back; come back," it said. He turned. It was his cellmate; he was looking up at him humbly, beseech-ingly, out of his inflamed eyes, with their red-drooping lower lids. The lock clanged again; 9009 turned with a spasm to the corridor. At its end, the door swung open; the five felons shot through it; 9009 saw their galloping backs rise and fall as those of jockeys at a race——

Then he straightened to his full height, swung his right arm across his cellmate's face, and with the roar of a bull, charged down the corridor.

Right away he had to leap. He had to leap the gray-haired

guard, looking upward with his scarlet-masked face; to leap the burglar, still gesticulating jerkily with his long-striped legs; a trusty, doubled up, coughing; another, paralyzed with fear. He leaped like a lean greyhound, he sped through the outer door, a ray of sun struck him hot on the cheek, he whipped around the corner into the wall-bound yard, he took three great strides—and stopped, facing six black disks.

They were gazing at him, round, swinging slowly from side to side, like the eyes of oxen, forty feet away, in a half circle converged upon him. After a while, behind the six black disks, he saw six dull-gleaming rifle-barrels, then behind the six dull-gleaming rifle-barrels, six brown stocks, then besides each stock, pressed close, a face, set, stone-like, and an eye, like a slit.

He stood there, with drooping jaw, his arms limp along his sides, while six blue-clad guards, each silent as a carven thing, aimed carefully at his breast, each with his index-finger upon his rifle-trigger.

0010

9009 waited to be shot, staring dully at the rifle-muzzles, then at the other things about him. His jaw drooped so that his mouth was half open, and his eyes were wide. He panted. Details came to him slowly.

Six guards, immobile, aiming their rifles at him.

Between him and the guards, two striped huddles, like wounded snakes upon the beaten earth of the place. A limp hand drooping loosely from the nearest huddle, a white face upturned, very still, a flash of yellow teeth between drawn lips—this was Miller. The other—he could not tell who the other was.

Off to one side, three more guards; in front of each, a convict; the guards holding drawn revolvers, each muzzle against the belly of one of the convicts. In the center of this group, breathing hard, a-snarl, the wiry little pickpocket.

Beyond, the gray high wall; and upon it, pacing slowly against a very blue sky, another guard, holding a rifle, loosely, like a hunter.

Six guards holding their rifles at him; three more holding drawn revolvers against three striped convicts; another guard on the wall—9009's eyes suddenly narrowed to slits.

A resonant clash of steel upon steel broke the panting silence. The cell-house door had been closed. Again a metallic clang: the inner door had been shut. Then, muffled,

 9009

a succession of dull slams, close one upon the other, that merged into a subdued roll as of thunder. The convicts within the cell-house were being locked up in their cells.

The six rifle-muzzles fell toward the ground; a footstep crunched behind; 9009 turned. It was Jennings.

The sallow face was heavy, expressionless; and the gray eyes were without light. One heavy hand, extending, grasped 9009's shoulder; the other explored his garments one after the other. "All right," said Jennings; "nothing on him." He turned his eyes upon 9009. "Thought you'd lam out, eh?" he said with the slightest sneer.

But 9009 did not answer. He was stupefied. And when Jennings ordered him come, he followed at a shambling gait, dazed, to the dungeon.

He sat there for several hours, on the steel floor, in the blackness, his hands hanging loose between his drawn-up knees. Gradually, out of the whirl of his mind, two pictures emerged. He saw Nichols, the confidence-man, walking slowly backward toward the inner corridor; he saw him shoot the burglar and run to his cell; he did not understand that. Then he saw himself bounding out into the yard—and stopping before six rifles; he did not understand that. His brain, anyway, was making but dull efforts to understand. All it did was this: it presented to him the two pictures, mechanically, passionlessly, as for inspection—the stony-faced confidence-man shooting the burglar from behind; the guards waiting outside to catch him as he came. He looked at these two pictures, stupid; he could not understand them.

He emerged from the dungeon at noon and was taken, blinking, into the sunny yard. Here a theatrical scene had been carefully arranged.

At a point midway between the door of the dining hall and the gates of the jute-mill lane, close to the stone-like track made by the thrice-daily march of the lock-step line, two deal tables had been placed side by side. And upon these tables, the three convicts killed in the break had been laid.

They had been dumped, not laid, dumped in their last attitudes, now frozen to rigidity. They sprawled in their stripes, ignoble with blood and earth, with limbs doubled under them or spread out, contorted, their faces, gray-white where they showed between bruise and clot, staring upward with glazed eyes upon which grains of dust lay without causing a blink. Miller leered, his long teeth showing yellow; the burglar's heavy jaw had fallen loosely upon his heavy throat, without hiding a black spot which spread down to the waist, coagulating the stripes; the third man lay arms spread as if crucified; he was a mere boy, and his face was serene.

"Look, you fellows, look!"

The voice of the captain, growling, was answered by the movement of the guards, pushing 9009, the pickpocket, and the other two men of the break closer to the tables. 9009 looked upon the heap. Miller leered at him with his yellow teeth; the burglar stared stupidly, with dropped jaw; the boy gazed upward with calm eyes, his mouth curved almost in a smile. 9009 remembered him now; he was a mountain boy and of late had taken to talking to himself.

An undercurrent of sound, a sort of attenuated whir, a buzzing that was dull, arose continuously. 9009 bent over, close; then he turned sick.

"Line 'em up," growled the captain.

To the right of the tables, 9009 was placed, erect; to the left of the tables, the other two. They formed a line, as for inspection. 9009 and the pickpocket, alive; then Miller, the burglar, and the boy, dead; then the other two convicts, alive. But the living men had dead faces.

They stood there, it seemed to them a long time. Above, the sky was very blue; the sun beat down upon their shaven heads; it poured perpendicularly upon the eyes of the dead men, which did not blink; and there was a still, warm silence, and underneath this still warm silence, a low steady buzzing. 9009 shuffled his feet. "Quiet!" growled the captain of the yard.

ch. ends p. 71

He stood before them, like a colonel before his spread regiment, looking at them with an inspecting frown; then a satisfaction smoothed his visage; "all right," he said to Jennings.

Jennings shouted down the yard; at the signal the gates of the jute-mill lane swung inward, and through the turreted arch in the wall the lock-step line emerged.

It came smoothly, in a lithe continuous flow, as if it were to be endlessly, through the arch, into the yard, undulating like a snake, gray as a larva, mounted upon legs like a centipede. A new eagerness seemed in its thousand limbs, a vague tremor was in its folds, its slight side-to-side motion seemed accelerated of rhythm; it came along the way, beaten to stone, that it had made through so many days, crawling from mill to hall and back again; it came, gray and flaccid, creeping forward with rapidity.

Then suddenly its head, as if catching a scent, went off the path in a long sidewise rear—a movement as that of a snake which would rear like a horse. There was a moment of disorder; the body and tail, pressing forward, knotted, vertebrae broke; the voices of the guards rose high and sharp—and then the head, with a gliding, submissive motion flattened out again, and came on, past the tables, the tables served with killed men that stared upward, flanked by live men with dead faces.

The line went by slowly. The guards, at the head, on the sides, delayed it with murmur and gesture, and the voice of the captain, growling, incessantly bade it look, look, look. It flowed by with its side-to-side swinging retarded of rhythm; one by one the white faces passed, glancing slantingly, deep-lined, heavy. Sometimes nostrils quivered slightly; sometimes prison pallor grayed. They passed in silence; in the warm still air there was no sound excepting the shuffling of feet, the low growl of the captain's voice bidding look, and the buzzing undertone. They passed, slit-eyed, stone-faced, sullen, and silent—9009 saw them all. He saw his little cellmate looking at him out of his inflamed eyes with that same shocked expression with which he had looked at him from his cell during the struggle in the corridor; he saw Hayes—and fantastically the shock-headed safecracker was still laughing the soundless sneering laugh he had laughed while looking out of his cell at 9009 during the break——

They passed by the four living men with dead faces, by the three dead men gazing at the sky—and one by one they sank into the door of the dining hall till the yard was desert again—except for the flanked tables, and the buzzing.

Then 9009 was taken back to the dungeon, and he was kept there for thirty days.

For thirty days he was in blackness and silence. At regular intervals, which were of twenty-four hours but seemed much longer, the wicket snapped open and a half loaf of bread with a pitcher of water was thrust in, entering with a gray pallor of daylight immediately shut off again. He slept much, in short periods, at any hour, irregularly; the rest of the time he squatted in the center of his cube of darkness, and thought. He saw the confidence-man, stepping back a-tiptoe, raising his arm, shooting; the burglar falling. He saw himself bounding down the corridor, leaping over white faces gazing upward, emerging out into the sunlight—into the bristling circle of the guards ambush. And now another picture had joined these two: he saw the shock-headed safecracker peering out of his cell and laughing his soundless sneering laugh during the struggle in the corridor; he saw his cellmate gazing at him with a shocked expression. And he did not understand.

At the end of thirty days he was taken before the Prison Board in the warden's office. There he faced two corporation lawyers whose corporations were then undergoing prosecution, a pig-eyed grocer who adulterated, a wholesale liquor merchant, and a wormy ward politician, and these men took his copper away from him.

He went back to the dungeon and thought. He saw the two smug corporation lawyers who taught their corporations

ch. ends next p.

how to sap the law, the pig-eyed grocer who sold pickles preserved in sulphuric acid, the wholesale liquor merchant who helped finance a corrupt municipal party and thus forced his whiskey on all the city saloons, the ward politician who paid for votes with dollars. He knew of these men; he had read their record. He saw them, sitting in a solemn line behind their desks, with an expression of shocked severity taking from him his copper. And suddenly his laugh rang harsh and loud between the steel walls.

He stayed in the dungeon thirty days longer. At regular intervals, which were of twenty-four hours, but seemed much longer, the wicket snapped open and, together with a pallor of day, there entered a half loaf of bread and a pitcher of water. He ate; he slept much, in short frequent periods, irregularly, stretched upon the cold steel floor. But the larger part of the time he thought. He saw the confidence-man shoot the burglar, he saw himself leaping into the ring of the guards ambush, he saw the leer of the safecracker, the shocked expression of his cellmate—and he did not understand.

On the twenty-fifth day the door opened and clanged shut again, and he was conscious of a presence there with him in the compressed darkness. He waited, silent, crouching; and after a while he heard a short, hard, dry cough.

"That you, pal?" he asked.

"Yes, it's me," answered the piping voice of his cellmate.

They were silent in the darkness. "What made you come in?" at length asked 9009.

"Got five days for talking in the line," said the invisible cellmate.

"What for did you do it?" pursued 9009.

"Thought they'd put me in this hole," admitted the thin voice. "I knowed you'd be feelin' like hell about bein' fooled."

"Fooled?" the voice of 9009 rose in a bellow.

"'Bout the framed-up break. Nichols, that bunco-man, he was the stool-pigeon that framed it for Jennings and the yard captain. Guess he'll get a pardon now. And 'Shorty' Hayes, he's laughing at ye; says you and he heard Jennings talk about the frame-up that time he and you was painting under the captain's window——"

The little man's voice died abruptly. 9009 had hurled himself upon the steel walls, and he was beating them with hands and feet, crushing his face against them in an effort to bite. He saw now. He saw himself, up on the painter's platform with 'Shorty' Hayes, hearing the words of Jennings floating out through the open window; he saw Nichols, the stony-faced confidence-man gradually preparing the break, and then, when it had come, killing the burglar; he saw the safecracker laughing at him from the door of his cell. He saw—and he beat madly with hands and feet and head. Like a maddened insect he whirled along the four walls of the dungeon, clawing, butting, rasping his teeth against the smooth impassive surface. Finally, exhausted, he stopped, crouching in the center of the cell. And after a while he laughed, a harsh laugh that rebounded dully from the walls of steel.

Then a hand fell on his shoulder; he felt the little cell-mate squatting by his side. His right hand went across his body; a small, hard paw seized it—and for hours, there, in the darkness, the two crouched silently side by side, hand in hand, without saying a word. At times 9009 laughed harsh and loud, and then the grip upon his hand tightened.

0011

9009 had turned.

He had changed faces as he had changed stripes. Among his kind he now moved a being apart, hard-eyed, cruel-mouthed, a line of sullen craft between his brows, a sneer at the end of his ugly lips. And he was feared. He was different, now, from the others; a developed brute more dangerous than they. Processes meant to break him had merely warped him; they had made of him the grimmest thing that walks—a convict without hope.

He wore red stripes, as the convict who had killed the garroter had done, as Miller the highwayman had done. These red stripes singled him out from the others. They displayed him as a red blotch in the long gray lock-step line; they flashed him out, a red target amid the gray groups in yard or cell-house or dining hall, to the guards pacing slow along walls or waiting in suspended cages with rifles loose in hand, like hunters. The red stripes meant this: that at the slightest disorder, the slightest tumult, the least suspicious movement or eddy in the mass of guarded criminals, it was he who was to receive the first bullets from the guards watching, rifles in hand, weary with monotonous vigil, and anxious to kill.

He worked in the foundry. Striped men made there stoves for thrifty housewives, and they were the desperate of the prison. The manufacture was simple. The convicts melted scrap in a furnace—a huge rusty-brown cylinder of iron, lined with firebrick, which stood at one end of the molding-room—then drew the molten metal and carried it in ladles to black-sand molds, where it hardened. The glowing viscous metal poured into these molds came forth rigid and black and shaped into parts, and the parts were put together into stoves. 9009 was a molder.

They were a black-faced scowling crew of felons, dumb at their toil, hating one another. Their striped suits, red-blotched with iron rust, were tattered; their heavy brogans gaped where molten drippings had burned away the leather. Some limped from burns, and some bore on hands and faces ugly sores—the marks of spattered liquid iron. They were savagely reckless at their work, and the guards had to watch them closely lest they maim themselves. They sweated in torment and strange wordless feuds existed among them; stealthy blows were struck without cause.

The molding room was long and low, earth-floored, dusky with shadows at noonday. On the earth floor, in rows flanking path-wide intervals, lay the molds—wooden frames about which was tamped black sand. Walls and roof were of corrugated iron. The naked rafters overhead were crusted with dirt; black dirt lay in thin layers on the window-panes and hung in cobwebbed festoons from the bars. At one end of the room, looming tall into the shadows until it became itself a shadow among them, stood the cylindrical furnace, gloomy when dead, and on pouring-off days a menacing monster which at sudden intervals vomited red-hot metal. In the center of the room, up among the dust-covered rafters, was a suspended steel-barred cage; and in it a guard stood, fingering his rifle. At the other end of the room, in the midst of a fiery spark shower, his black face catching weird high lights from the glowing rain about him, Jimmy Carroll, the little cellmate, sat on a high stool at the emery wheel. Often 9009 glanced over there, especially toward night, when the little man swayed sickly on his perch.

Four days a week 9009 tamped black sand about the mold-patterns. He worked, pounding, pounding, pounding, with loose shoulders, the cold smell of earth, charcoal, and fresh iron dust in his nostrils; somber-lined faces and striped forms flitted about him; at times his eyes, unconsciously rising, gave him a glimpse of the cage overhead, with the guard vague within, or of his cellmate, swaying on his high stool in a Sodom-like rain. Two days a week he stood in line with the other molders, holding his long-handled ladle and waiting his turn to slip it under the sullen red stream which the furnace gave. On these pouring-off days, the sweating felons strained like black-faced demons among lurid glows, emerging from deep shadows into abrupt flares and dropping back into their depths. They looked like men long dead and damned for all time. But always, to 9009, a glimpse of his cellmate, swaying on his high stool in a fiery rain, came as a subtle respite.

When one of the convicts was hurt, the others laughed. And one of the jests of the molding-room was to spit into your neighbor's filled ladle, causing an explosion that seared him. A felon did this to 9009 one day. 9009 leaped upon him, and when he was dragged off, he was trampling the prostrate form of the evil jester.

For this he went to the dungeon for ten days. When on the morning terminating his sentence he re-entered the foundry and looked up toward the emery wheel, Jimmy Carroll was not there. Another convict sat at his place, in the fiery shower.

All that day, tamping black sand into wooden patterns, 9009 questioned about him, questioned with sharp glances from shifting eyes—but he got no answer.

That night he was all alone in his cell, and all night he pondered. In the morning, during cleaning-up time, he began again his questioning, furtive, lipless, but fiercer every moment; but again only shaken heads and shrugging shoulders met him.

For a week it was thus. He was alone in his cell at night; in

ch. ends p. 78

the daytime a strange convict sat at the emery wheel—a long, lean man with a lead-hued face. And the toil was harder than it had been before—and his savage questioning, insistent and implacable, rebounded from the hard faces of his fellows as from blank stone walls.

Then, after a time, a rumor began to percolate slowly through the prison—in lipless words, from stone face to stone face, vague, incomplete at first, irritating as the tapping snatches of a telegraph receiver out of order, but little by little, in that mysterious way rumor has, growing more detailed, surer, more complete.

Jimmy Carroll the little cellmate was dead. He had been shot.

This was all for a time; then by glance, by shrug, by swiftly stolen word, 9009 was directed to "Shorty" Hayes, the shock-headed safecracker who had laughed at him as he had joined the break. And one Sunday he cornered him in the yard and drew the whole story from him.

This convict was under a fifty years' sentence. He had lost his copper long since. Now he was to get it back from the Governor of the State. In some subtle subterranean way he had got hold of the facts of Jimmy Carroll's death, and the knowledge was worth to him his copper.

He crowed harshly over this, long, before he told 9009 anything. And while telling, every sentence or two he broke from the telling and croaked again his triumph. "They're a-goin' to get me me copper back from the Governor," he would croak; "thirteen years' copper they're a-goin' to give me back—fer what I know. Fer what I know," he repeated, chuckling raspingly. "Ho-ho-ho, me copper fer what I know!"

What he knew, what he had gained in some mysterious way, was this:

Two mornings after 9009's fight, and while he was in the dungeon, Jimmy Carroll suddenly had refused to work.

He had been taken to the office of the captain of the yard. And there, quietly, stubbornly, he had again refused to work.

They had taken him, then, to the whipping-post in the chapel.

"Put your hands up to the ring," said the captain, pointing to the ring, stapled into the post a little more than man-height, to which the hands of the victim were manacled during the flogging.

"I won't," said the little black-faced man; "I'm sick; I won't work; and I won't be flogged."

"Put up your hands," said the captain.

"I won't; I'm sick and I won't be flogged."

"Put up your hands," said the captain, picking up the cat.

"I won't," said the little black-faced man, folding his arms upon his caved-in chest.

The captain's face went very white. "Jennings," he said to the guard standing by; "Jennings, you get your rifle."

Jennings had disappeared, then had returned with the rifle.

"Put your hands up to this ring," began the captain again when Jennings, rifle in hand, again stood in the chapel.

"I won't," said the little man. He stopped to cough, looking up at the captain out of his inflamed eyes, with their red-drooping lower lids. "You c'n kill me; I won't be flogged."

"Carroll, I'm man of my word," said the captain, very white. "And so help me God, if you don't put up your hands to this ring, you'll be shot."

"Shoot," said Jimmy Carroll.

"Jennings, get ready," said the captain.

Jennings stared at him, stared at Carroll, raised his rifle, and aimed it at the little black-faced man.

"Now, put up your hands," said the captain, his face suddenly going black as the little man's.

"I won't," said the little man.

"Shoot," said the captain.

And Jennings had shot. And Jimmy Carroll had gone over backward in a thin little sprawl, a bullet in his heart.

"And now," said the safecracker, his face, suddenly very

ch. ends next p.

sinister, bent close to 9009's; "now Buddy, remember, I'll cut off your head if ye open yer mouth!"

But 9009 did not answer. He sat there, his eyes upon the ground, long. And the next day, from the machine-shop of the foundry, he stole a big heavy file, just such a file as, months before, he had seen the red-striped convict of the jute-mill plunge into the shoulders of the garroter. And that night, through the long sleepless hours, he stretched deliciously to the rasp of it against his flesh, there beneath his red-striped jacket, upon his heart.

0012

About the rasp-file 9009's life now enwrapped itself. The thing was the symbol of his purpose, his engrossing purpose, the one fixed light left in his blackened soul. For many days he carried it with him just as it was, beneath his garments; at night he stretched deliciously to its rasp, there against his skin, upon his heart. A somnolent apathy had come over him; that mere contact gave him a profound satisfaction, almost a satiety: it was with an effort that he roused himself to the next step. But at length he stole from the machine-shop another file, a small one, of diamond steel, and with it he began to sharpen the big one, of softer steel, into a knife.

He worked at night, surreptitiously, with infinite precaution, under the muffle of his blanket, his ears taut to the hissing feet of the guard; and progress was slow, but exquisite from its very slowness. He was greatly delayed by the necessity of parting for long periods with the object of his tenderness.

He had found, in the stone wall of the laundry, which stood a bare two feet from the stone wall of the cook-house, a niche hollowed for a water-pipe; and whenever he feared discovery, or his instinct announced to him the coming of a search, he dropped his file in the niche behind the water-pipe. Then for days he would be separated from it, tortured with sudden accesses of fear in spite of his confidence in the security of his hiding-place. But he had become wonderfully patient, and he stood the test well. His purpose burned within him always, without a sputter, fixed, unalterable. He remembered how the murderer of the garroter had waited, days, weeks, months, never letting the desire of his heart light up his eyes, while the garroter passed and repassed him, and on his breast the knife lay, not quite ready. A patience such as this was now with him always, a patience he felt inexhaustible within him, and in which he took a grim and sullen pride.

And so, night after night, with intervals of long separations, he fondled the file, and beneath his caressing and firm sculpturing gradually it grew into the shape he loved—pointed, razor-edged, well-poised. The feel of its well-balanced weight in his hand was a constant joy. It could split a skull or carve out a rib. It was just like the knife he had watched on the desk of the captain of the yard, the day of the jute-mill murder, a trifle bigger, stronger, better shaped if anything. It cut him often as it lay against his skin, upon his heart—and he accepted these wounds voluptuously, as a mother accepts the scratches of the babe she loves; at night he stretched ecstatically to the rasping of it, as a religious fanatic stretches to the torture of his hair shirt. Visions came to him then. He saw the red-striped convict of the jute-mill spring, leap-frog fashion, upon the garroter; he saw his right hand sink into the bent back with a crunch, then rise, fall, rise, fall. And by a swift transformation, it was he that sprang, leap-frog fashion; his hand that pumped, up and down, up and down; his knees that grasped a thick gurgling neck—and the neck was not that of the garroter.

He waited, grimly patient, day after day, week after week. At times, without much conviction, he tried to coax on the favorable moment; and this resulted in what the prison officials took for attempts at escaping—attempts incredibly stupid.

On one Sunday, for instance, he wandered into the office of the captain of the yard under the excuse of drawing a new suit of underwear. He could hear the voice of Jennings in the inner office, and he was very long in picking his garment, rejecting suit after suit under flimsy pretexts; then, after finally he had to choose, loitered in the outer corridor, aimlessly, till Wilson, with the unerring instinct of the informer, becoming suspicious, ordered him out. He cursed Wilson; and for this he was given a week in the dungeon.

On another day, he broke up the lock-step line in its morning march from cell-house to dining hall. Jennings commanded the line that day. He stood near the wall, fifty feet from the line as it passed. With a furtive movement, 9009 threw from him a piece of plug tobacco which he had traded from another convict for a pair of hoarded shoelaces. It lit on the ground, twenty feet from Jennings, unseen of all. Then, very calmly, 9009 stepped out of the line and walked toward Jennings. Immediately voices rose; from the wall a rifle cracked; a bullet struck the ground at 9009's feet. Disdainfully he stooped, picked up the tobacco, placed it between his teeth, and shuffled back to the line. He had been unable to get nearer than the twenty feet from Jennings.

For this he was given the water-cure. Fettered to a ring stapled in the stone wall of the corridor leading to the dungeon, he stood before the captain of the yard, who played upon his face the powerful stream of a hose till he was half-drowned and chilled to the marrow.

Sometime after he made another attempt, a more serious one, but just as stupid from the point of view of the prison officers. Slipping out of the line as it left the foundry (it was the dusk of a winter's day) he crawled to the cook-house and slipped into the narrow space between that and the laundry, near the niche where he used to hide his knife at times of danger from search. By the mouth of this narrow gut,[1] Jennings had to pass four times a day on his way to the jute-mill and back.

But Jennings did not appear. He was out at the head of a

---

[1] A gut is a thin, tight passageway.

posse which, deceived, pursued an unwitting tramp over the hills. For three days 9009 crouched foodless and shelterless in his retreat while manhunters roamed the hills for him on the outside; then Wilson, heading a search within the walls, found him. For his pains he was throttled almost to death before the guards could part 9009's iron fingers.

For this 9009 was formally tried in the court of the district under the charge of assault to commit murder. The trial was short. 9009 did not open his mouth once. And he moved not a muscle when the judge sentenced him to ten additional years in the penitentiary.

He was placed, now, in solitary confinement.

The solitary cells were on the top floor of the building to which the garroter had pointed, for the information of the murderer, on 9009's first day. This building was known about the prison as the "Stone Building," probably from the massiveness of its walls. The solitary cells were in a corridor by themselves. The light was dim there; it came from a single small window high up in the wall.

They watched him, in his cage up there, in the shadowy corridor; a guard stood all day before his steel-barred door. By night he was left alone. The cell was steel-walled, steel-floored, steel-barred in front. It was six feet long and five wide. The bunk took two and a half feet of the width; so there was left a space six feet long and two and a half feet wide in which 9009 could walk. Once each two weeks his guard took him into the corridor and let him exercise there. His eyes dilated with the dim light. His hair had grown long, for they seldom sent the prison barber to him, and the lines on his face had deepened to crevasses.

He slept, fitfully, as an animal sleeps in a cage, by short snatches; he walked to and fro in the confined space; he mended his clothes. And he planned.

To merely wait for his chance, now, was not sufficient. To fulfill his purpose, he must get out of the solitary cell. His knife lay in the niche behind the water-pipe; he had dropped it there when discovered by Wilson. For the fulfillment of his purpose, he must have the knife; and to have the knife he must get out of his cell. The rest would be comparatively easy, for the building was not locked. It would take care and stealth, a careful avoidance of guard and trusty.

He felt no hurry. The years of his new sentence lay ahead of him; he took pleasure in a contemplation of them, stretching long before him; it was as if eternity, suddenly, had been placed at the service of his purpose. Once only did he sicken with impatience and worry; this was when lipless prison rumor told him that Jennings lay ill in the hospital. Two weeks later, though, he heard that the guard was back at his duty in the jute-mill, and his bars roared out his relief in a rattle that reverberated long in the dusky corridor. But this had been a lesson; he saw the danger of procrastination, and concentrated his mind on the problem of leaving his cell. And finally the solution came.

He began to ask for needles often—as often as he dared, making the while a great show of repairing his garments. In this way, in a year he collected ten needles.

He took these ten needles and fitted them into the wooden stem of a brier pipe.[2] He fitted them close together, like the teeth of a comb; they were hard; they made a diminutive saw; and they bit steel. With these needles he began to saw his bars.

He sawed for a year, and had three bars nearly through; and then his cell was changed.

His patience, now, had become something fundamental within him, as granite is fundamental of the earth. He sat down and waited. They changed him again to another cell. And then to another. He spent nearly three years in different cells, and then, one morning, he found himself again in the cell where he had sawed. That night he tested the bars. They were as he had left them, three years before. Three of them

---

[2] A tobacco pipe made from the roots of a large woody plant of the heath family.

ch. ends next p.

were severed but for a thread of steel; the guards had discovered nothing. He began purring at the fourth bar.

He worked craftily, with stealth, at night, very slowly; for before him lay years, the eternity of time placed, by a trick of Fate, at the disposal of his purpose; and it was silly to take chances. He worked in the shadows, crouched, rubbing evenly, quietly, but firmly, cutting bars of steel with needles. When he had done each night, he scattered with deep breaths of his lungs the almost imperceptible little heap of steel dust resulting, and smudged over the thin wound in the bar with a bit of moistened bread and lampblack.[3] So he lived, eating but little, sleeping fitfully, like a caged animal, lying on his back staring up into the shadows with eyes dilated with long penetration of gloom, lived with his purpose. But at times an agony of cold sweat poured out upon his skin as he thought that perhaps his knife, his precious file-knife, needle-pointed, razor-edged, so well balanced, toward which he was cutting his way through bars of steel with needles, that his knife might not be there, in the niche behind the water-pipe, where he had left it.

And then, suddenly, one day an astounding thing happened; he received a letter.

Two convicts, two new trusties whom 9009 had never seen, were cleaning the corridor. The arm of one snapped abruptly, and between the bars something that looked like a white butterfly fluttered in and lit upon the steel floor near 9009. He placed his foot upon it, and several minutes later picked it up.

It was a letter, and it was from Nell. It was from Nell! From Nell, the woman he had kept from his thoughts, the woman from whom, stubbornly, knowing life and her kind, he had refused to expect anything; and it was an extraordinary letter.

For three years she had been working from the outside to help him. And now she had accomplished her purpose.

---

[3] A black pigment made from soot.

In the passageway between the bakery and the laundry, the letter said, in an old drain-pipe, a rifle, a revolver, and a rope lay cached for him.

That night 9009 sawed with his needles through the last fibers of the four bars.

0013

It was the dark hour before the dawn, black and still and cold, when 9009, slipping the last severed bar from its place and laying it noiselessly down, wiggled out of his cell like a red-barred snake. A moment later he was outside the building, shrinking, a shadow among shadows.

He was in the upper yard. To his right was the "Stone Building" from which he had just emerged; to his left, across the yard, lay his old cell-house. Before him, a hundred feet away, opened the alley-way leading to the lower yard with its little garden, where were the warden's office and the sleeping quarters of the guards. The left side of this alley was made by the second cell-house and the dining hall; the right side by the line of outhouses. These consisted of the laundry, the cook-house, and bakery. Between them were narrow spaces, mere guts two feet wide. It was in the nearer of these that he had once hidden for three days; in the same one was the niche where his knife lay; and the farther one was now his goal. Between this and the point where now he stood was a stretch of the yard, a hundred feet of it, bluely aglare with the lights of the electric mast.

Everything was very still where he stood, and very somber. Behind him was a stretch of wall—and on it a muffled guard walked slowly, carrying his gun loosely in his right arm, like a hunter. In the center of the yard, high on a slim mast, a cluster of arc-lights threw frozen blue-rays wide into the sea of darkness below. They revealed harshly everything they touched: the beaten path in the yard, the stones of the high granite wall, the guard, his rifle-barrel gleaming cold, the "Stone Building," hard and high, the cell-house, black-patched with barred windows, the cluster of out-houses before him, and especially, with a frigid intensity, an uncompromising malevolence, the stretch of beaten ground between him and his goal.

He stood in the narrow gutter of shadow along the base of the facade of the "Stone Building," and he stared at the guard on the wall with dilated eyes used to searching darkness. The man was coming from the far extremity of his beat, toward 9009, pacing slowly, his rifle loose in hand; he paused to readjust the muffler around his neck, and then, abruptly, his head snapped forward and his rifle rose in his hand.

It may have been the pillar of shade, the blacker shadow in the black shadows which had not been there before—for peering straight toward the place, the guard became very tense; in the glare 9009 could see his features tighten, his left arm crook. The rifle was still going up; it stopped half-way between hip and shoulder; the two men stood still as graven images—the guard, a sharp figure in the blue-white light, bent, taut, watching; the barred convict in the shadow, crouching, motionless, his eyes peering without lid move-ment, like the pitiless eyes of a snake.

And then the guard relaxed; he dropped back his rifle to the old loose carriage and resumed his walk. 9009, immo-bile, unblinking, watched him approach the end of his beat and then, pivoting, start for the other end, his back turned; instantly he slid out into the luminous space.

He ran, swiftly and silently, on the balls of his feet, his arms half doubled, his chin thrown upon his humped right shoulder, looking backward all the time at the guard upon the wall, who paced along with his back still turned. He cov-ered forty feet—and the guard still walked; fifty, sixty—the guard was slowing up; seventy feet the guard paused. There in the middle of the walk something, perhaps some cold premonition, had arrested him. His gun flashed; he was turning. Throwing his eyes forward, 9009 leaped in great bounds; the shadow of the dining hall, sharp as the tape at the end of a race, cut the ground ten feet ahead. He gave a last look backward; the guard whipped around; 9009 plunged head-first, like a frog, and sprawled upon his belly within the darkness which immediately closed about him like water.

He lay as he had fallen, awaiting the shock of the bullet, the roar of the guard's rifle. But he did not move. He could not believe that he had not been seen. A moment passed. A desire to draw up his legs possessed him; he knew that they must be out, distinct, in the light. But he did not move. He lay like a stone. His face was in the earth; he could taste mud upon his lips; his feet felt cold as though he were beneath a blanket and they were sticking out; he imagined them enormously visible. But he did not move.

A minute passed, a century. But there was no shock of bullet, no roar of rifle. Finally, he turned his head.

He turned it slowly, smoothly, until he could look at right angles to his body, then with infinite precautions, in imperceptible progressions, he bent it till the line of vision had passed his shoulder. But still he could see nothing. Something opaque and enormous barred his way; an immense pillar. It was barred. It was his arm.

He moved the arm in toward his side with the same smooth stealthiness—and he could see across the lit earth of the yard, clear to the wall. But he could not see the top of the wall. Again he began an infinitely cautious movement. He raised his head, from the neck, with no body change, as though he were a contortionist; the muscle of his throat cracked with the effort.

And then he saw. The guard was pacing back along the beat his gun loose in hand, his back turned.

ch. ends p. 95

9009 now crawled, on his belly like a red-ringed snake, into the alleyway.

He crawled by the narrow gut where his knife had lain hidden for more than three years, and went on, writhing, to the second, between the cook-house and bakery. Crouching at the entrance of this, he looked back. He could not see the guard; and he must be invisible to the guard. He rose and went in between the two buildings, squeezing edgewise, his right hand ahead, feeling the wall, until it came against the broken drain-pipe. He dropped his hand into the pipe—and the cold muzzle of a rifle, there between his fingers, thrilled him to the marrow.

He stood there, his hand in the pipe, his fingers about the cold muzzle, long; then with a jerk drew up the rifle. It fell across his outstretched arms, and he held it thus a moment, as a mother holds her child, his eyes examining it swiftly, passing with satisfaction over the thin, short barrel, the massive breech-lock, the stock, heavy with stored death. The magazine was full, a cartridge was in the breech—he knew that those who had climbed the wall and hidden it had been negligent of no such details. He took up the weapon in his hands now, right hand about small of stock, left hand a sliding crotch about the barrel—and suddenly he snapped up to his full height.

A terrific feeling of power had risen through him. Once, in this prison, he had been a man intent on obedience; months had changed him to a sullen suspicious convict; years had made of him a crouching, stalking beast; and now, at the touch of this rifle, he sprang up a monster. His muscles were of steel, his nerves were of iron; he was sure of himself, absolutely sure. He felt that he could kill, that no one, not God Himself, could keep him from killing. He could kill when he pleased. He could not miss, of that he was incredibly sure; in his arms, already, in his arms, in his eye, in his trigger-finger, he had the feel of the coming kills.

He groped again into the pipe; his hands found three

things: first, a rope, coiled, at one end of which dangled a grappling hook; then a revolver, then a box of ammunition. He coiled the rope about his waist. The revolver was a long heavy single-action six-shooter, of the pattern he had always liked. He tucked it beneath his waistband. The cartridges he dropped, loose, into one of his pockets. Then he stood, erect, in the alley, close to the wall of the cook-house.

Dawn was coming in the east, a sullen dawn. It colored lightly the scale-tips of a mackerel sky, and then, with weird swiftness, painted perpendicularly three great red bars across the murky horizon. 9009, standing in the shadowy alley, saw the three red bars; he knew that in half an hour the day guards would be up, that in half an hour the whole prison would be rising—and a sudden temptation convulsed him.

He saw the guard, alone, upon the wall; an impulse told him to shoot, rush to the wall, climb, jump, rush to freedom, now, on the instant, using the moment's opportunity. His heart stabbed him with a palpitation, his blood leaped through his veins—and the stock of his rifle sprang to his shoulder.

He stood thus, a long minute, the stock smooth against his cheek, peering, through the crotch of the back-sight, at the white bead held immobile against the dark loom of the guard's breast, his finger, twitching, crooked about the trigger, while he fought the fight. Finally, with a release of pent-up breath, he lowered the gun. The temptation was gone; his purpose had won; again it was with him, grim, inflexible, unconquerable.

He crept into the narrow gut between the laundry and the cook-house, and in the niche behind the water-pipe found his file-knife where he had laid it, three years before. The blade was rusty now, dulled with cakes of rust; the point was gone and was like a knob; but the thing still was hard and thick and heavy; its well-balanced weight was still a joy in the hand. He slipped it under his waistband, by the revolver— and immediately, like a memory of old times, almost sweet,

ch. ends p. 95

he felt the rasp of it upon his skin, the rasp that once had been a promise, the promise now so near of fulfillment. He crept back farther into the narrow passage, and waited there, patient, alone with his purpose.

The whole heavens were red now, deep red, like congealing blood. A cold light spread along the ground, sweeping, swift, silent. In the blackness of the gut, 9009 listened. He caught the vague stir of awakening men in the cell-house. The stir grew, became detached and distinct noises. Doors rang, a tread of feet sounded, footsteps came down the alley; two trusties passed, paused in front of the cook-house, coughing shiveringly, then entered. He heard the rasp of a match, a clang of stove-lids, and then voices, muffled, within. In a few minutes the day guards would be dressed. The mackerel sky above settled to a cold drab; 9009 stepped out silently into the alley-way.

He stood there a moment, erect and motionless; then his rifle leaped to his shoulder, bellowed, and the blue-clad guard upon the wall toppled over, hung on the edge an instant, and slid along the perpendicular stones to a huddle in the yard.

And 9009 stepped out full into the yard, red-striped, gaunt, and terrible. He walked slowly, on the balls of his feet, his body inclined forward from the waist, his chin, pivoting upon his neck, thrusting itself out to the right, to the left, as he strode; and in his right hand his rifle, held loosely, like a hunter's.

The reverberation of the shot was still bounding from building to building, mingled with the echo of a shout which had followed. A shrill whistling now rose, strident, into the air. A white-faced trusty ran out of the cook-house; another. 9009 kept on, going down the middle of the yard, slowly, looking to right and to left. A trusty showed his head at the door of the cell-house. 9009 shot him, wantonly, gleefully, full in the face—a long shot, but he could not miss, he felt he could not miss, never miss. A flick of dust sprang from the ground at his feet, over his head a brief snarl passed, almost simultaneously the cracks of two rifles rang heavy between the walls; he grinned and pumped a new cartridge into the breech of his gun.

And then he began to run; going low, he made for the "Stone Building." The rifles cracked again; bullets struck to his right and to his left. He reached the end of the "Stone Building," halted, gave a swift look, then sprang forward toward the wall with a great self-announcing yell. He reached the wall, shot along it like a rabbit, then, when he was out of sight of the men above, quietly slipped back into the shadow of the "Stone Building." A laugh cleft his face as he saw the guards upon the wall, back toward him, peering still in the direction from which he had doubled. Then, in successive furtive rushes, he slid back to the alley and crouched in the narrow gut between cook-house and bakery, waiting.

He had accomplished three things by these movements. By shooting the guard upon the wall, he had aroused the whole prison, including all the other guards; by his feigned rush to the wall, he had determined just to what point these awakened guards should throw themselves in the first impulse of the alarm; by his circuitous doubling back, he now stood where they must all pass.

In spite of his running, he was breathing steadily; his muscles were like steel; and he was absolutely sure of himself, of his power to kill. He laid down his rifle and drew his revolver. He waited there, all alone with his purpose, peering out of the black gut. The whole prison, now, was buzzing about him like a beehive. Shouts sounded, gruff, like orders. A guard passed by on the run, his face very red; two more, putting on their coats as they ran; a whole group of five. He still waited. There was an interval of silence; again the drum of approaching feet. He peered—and then he glided out into the center of the alley and faced Jennings.

The guard stopped in the middle of a step; and the two

ch. ends next p.

men stood there alone in the desert alley, in the wan light of morning, facing each other, looking into each other's eyes.

The guard was half-dressed, his shirt open on his hairy chest, his suspenders hanging behind. His eyes narrowed, then widened; a flicker of light for an instant sprang into them, then died at once, leaving them as of old, lidless, opaque, white-gray; and his sallow face showed no emotion, though slowly, like an invisible blush, a dull threat rose in it. 9009 red-barred, stood with coarse-shod feet close together, bending slightly forward from the waist, his revolver at the end of his arm, held with crooked elbow close to his ribs; and in his face, gray with the prison pallor, his two eyes glowed like fires at the bottom of two caves.

They stood thus, it seemed long, motionless. Then the guard straightened his shoulders, and he half smiled. Immediately he was very serious again; and then he spoke.

"Put down that gun," he said, calmly, evenly.

The upper lip of 9009 raised like a theater-curtain and showed his teeth. It remained raised.

"Drop that gun," said Jennings again, his voice like furbished steel; and a film came over his eyes.

But 9009 was not listening; he was absorbed in another problem. He was trying to decide how he would kill Jennings. His first impulse had been to shoot him through the heart. Then he had wanted to put out with bullets the white-gray eyes. Then he had almost made up his mind to shoot him low in the body, so that he would die slowly and in great pain. But as he stood there, frigid, gun in hand, a profound dissatisfaction of these methods had filled his being. Somehow, none fitted; they were discordant, all of them, with a dream he had dreamed.

"Put down that gun," said Jennings for the third time.

And then 9009 knew.

He stooped, laid down the gun upon the ground, and snatched at his waistband. He rose to a crouch, to full height, and his right arm, unfolding, continued the upward movement. He stood thus a moment, motionless, straight, shoulders back, head back, right hand high in air. Then Jennings, bending, rushed forward, and 9009 sprang upon him.

He sprang high, leap-frog fashion; his left hand snapped down Jennings's lowered head with a jerk, and now the other hand, still high in air, whistled down. It sank into the guard's back with a crunch. It rose, fell, rose, fell, rose and fell, rose and fell, rose and fell in a rapid crescendo of pumping movement, crunching into the heap beneath long after it had become limp.

Then 9009, springing lithely to his feet, flung the file-knife from him in a wide gesture, and picking up his rifle, strode for the wall.

0014

9009 picked up his rifle and made for the wall. There were two guards upon it at the point which he chose, holding their rifles in both hands, like hunters waiting for a flock of quail to rise, and they fell to the double crack of his rifle ere[1] they could pull a trigger. One dropped inside the yard, the other hung, quivering, on the edge of the wall. Unwinding the rope around his waist, 9009 threw the grappling iron across the rail of the guards walk, and hurling his rifle ahead of him, climbed swiftly up like an ape. He paused for the flicker of an instant, there on the top, the inside of the prison like a diagram beneath him, the guard, now still, at his feet; then, disdainful of the rope, sprang down. He lit, huddled, by his rifle, seized it, and then, hunch-backed, ran for the hill. Shots sounded as he climbed, bullets whined by him, but he reached the summit, dived over it, and scrambled into the broad road at the point whence, years before, his coupled wrist raised by the garroter's pointing hand, he had had first sight of the prison's turreted walls. 9009 stopped and looked.

It was near winter, but the drought of the lingering fall had left the land arid, and the rounded hill still rose tawny against the sky. The prison was changed. A consternation brooded in its battlemented facades; within, men were running to

---

[1] Before.

and fro, criss-crossing, aimlessly; and from the guards wall, near a turret, three trusties were lowering a limp, blue form. Behind and above, like a red eye crooked in its orbit, the dead sun looked. Throwing both hands up into the air and brandishing his rifle, John Collins let out a shrill whoop of defiance and hate; then, turning, plunged on down the hill.

To the south, gray beneath a gray sky, lay the bay, whipped up into sudden bursts of livid fury by cold squalls. Collins kept it to his left and made for the edge of the chaparral[2] lining a patch of forest to the west. If he could gain this, the immediate pursuit would end, and there would be an interval of rest before the systematic manhunt would begin. He ran across the hills, crackling dry with the drought, a strange, red-striped animal whose eyes flashed, who bent and ducked and crouched and sought hollows. Once only did he stop; this to the drumming approach of a guard, who had been able to obtain a horse. From the top of a knoll where he lay flat, Collins shot down the guard, then went on, leaving the well-trained horse standing with long bridle dropped to the ground by his rider's reclining form. The halt had given him a glimpse of other blue-clad guards scattered over the land to the rear; he threw himself on with fresh impetus, and it was gasping, with veins swollen, that he reached the fringe of the chaparral just as the sun, definitively breaking through the veil of morning vapors, began to pour its yellow heat pitilessly upon the yellow land.

He went on straight till among the pines, then turned to the right toward the north. The city, which was his goal, lay to the south; yet till noon, for ten miles, he traveled straight north. During that time he showed himself only three times.

The first time was at a farmhouse—a small, weather-beaten house in the center of a clearing, to which he came just after the breakfast hour. A clatter of dishes, the song of a woman's voice, met him as he approached. He stood in the

---

[2] Vegetation consisting chiefly of tangled shrubs and thorny bushes.

doorway, red-barred, sullen-jawed, the rifle in hand; and the song died in a high quaver.

"Gimme food," he growled; "quick!"

The woman stared at him, white-faced, the dish that she had been wiping held tight against her breast. He scowled; the dish fell to the floor in twenty fragments.

"Quick!"

Without a word, she turned to the pantry.

"An' don't squeak," he went on; "if ye do, I'll cut your head off."

She placed the food before him on the table—bread, meat, potatoes, milk, a pot of lukewarm coffee. He gulped it down like a dog, watching all the time the woman through narrowed lids. Once, at some noise in the yard, he took up his rifle and glided a-tiptoe to the window. He stood there a moment, peering out; meanwhile, the woman took hold of the table with both hands, leaning forward heavily, her eyes closed; but as he turned and went back to the food, she stood up again, very stiff.

When he had done eating, he crammed under his jacket the meat and bread that remained, strode out, and vanished in the woods.

An hour later he heard the sound of an axe. He crept toward it through the undergrowth and saw a wood-chopper working over a fallen log. The man's shirt was open on his chest; his face was red and shiny, and at each stroke he uttered a sound between a grunt and a shout. "Huh-huh-huh," he said as he chopped. Collins rose before him as the axe rose—and the wood-chopper became a statue poised with axe high in air.

"Put down that axe," Collins growled.

The chopper dropped the axe.

"Now, take off your clothes," said Collins. The chopper began to strip. But when he had pulled off his shirt, an abrupt change came over him. "Say, what's the matter with you, eh? What's the matter with you?" he shouted.

ch. ends p. 106

His face was aflame, his eyes glistened; he doubled up his fists. Instantly the fists loosened and sprang high over his head as with a smart tap the muzzle of Collins's rifle settled against his stomach. "Oh, all right, all right," he said in subdued tone; "all right, all right, don't shoot." Then slowly, as if in an aside directed to the trees: "For God's sake!"

A moment later Collins crashed out through the brush clad in the garments of a workingman, leaving the wood-chopper in the clearing, naked before a striped huddle at which he gazed with indecision and disgust.

These short apparitions, Collins found, had been sufficient to his plan. The chase was pressing up northward. Once, throwing himself into the ditch beside the county road, he let pass two blue-clad guards on horseback, going swiftly, bent forward in their saddles. Later, from a knoll he saw a whole sheriff's posse trot by, shining with newly distributed badges, clattering with weapons—sawed-off shotguns, repeating rifles, six-shooters. The bead of his gun was upon the little band, playfully springing from one to the other, but he did not shoot.

He came upon them again at noon, in a little town consisting of a general merchandise store, a saloon, a post office, and a huddle of cottages. They were gathered in a picturesque group on the high wooden sidewalk in front of the saloon, tilted back on rawhide chairs, or standing about with clanging spurs, their rifles against the wall, their horses tied to the rack in the street, a circle of admiring urchins about them. The leader, a big, jovial man, was speaking vociferously amid a popping of small boastful interruptions, when Collins, gun in hand, chin thrust forward, walked in down the middle of the main street. A small boy, with a shout, raised his arm, pointing; the men sprang to their feet.

And then, right from the hip, Collins' rifle cracked; the big, jovial man pitched forward on his face. The rifle leaped to Collins' shoulder, and with his right arm suddenly limp, another man of the group staggered into the saloon. Behind him the rest of the posse jammed, fighting to get in. Only one made for the rifles, stacked against the wall, and Collins toppled him over just as his hand was upon the nearest. Running low, Collins made for the horses. He untied them, scattered them, all but one, with a fusillade from his revolver, sprang upon the one he held, and galloped out of the town—still going north. Two miles away, he led the horse down the bed of a brook into a ravine, tied him to a tree, and then, afoot, doubled back toward the south, toward the city, his goal, at last.

He traveled the rest of the day as few men have ever traveled—running, leaping, walking swiftly, always silent, always flitting forward without rest. Only twice did he stop, to watch from some hiding-place, along the barrel of his rifle, posses going by; one was led by the sheriff who six years before had taken him to the prison, a grizzly fellow with a long mustache, and wearing a sombrero; both times the posses were going northward, so that he had to master his desire to kill. Dusk came, and he pressed on, reeking with sweat, but unweary, the monstrous glare-dome of the city ahead. Finally, the glow resolved itself into details, and he trotted in between two rows of street-lamps.

Almost immediately he came upon a policeman. The man, a big, burly hulk, was walking slowly, twirling his stick, his helmet slightly tilted back. Collins dropped into a blind alley.

"Here, come out of there, you," growled the policeman, half jocosely;[3] "come out, come on, I want to see you!"

Collins stepped out and without raising his arm shot him. The policeman sat down with an astonished expression, coughed, and lay back on the sidewalk. Collins went on at a rapid silent walk to the next street, and, turning, ran. To his ear came the shrill affrighted cry of a police whistle. From the right another came; from the left. He ran, smoothly and carefully, his ears taut to the rasping whistles, his eyes piercing the shadows ahead.

---

[3] Playfully; humorously.

ch. ends p. 106

A milk-wagon rattled across his way as he came to a corner. He sprang toward it; the muzzle of his rifle touched the driver. The man drew in, and Collins leaped up by his side. They rattled noisily down the deserted streets wanly lit up by rare gas-lamps. The whistlings dwindled, ceased. Several times they passed policemen, frozen figures upon their beats. Collins's rifle lay beneath the seat, but the muzzle of his revolver, all the time, was against the ribs of the driver, who handled the reins to Collins's fierce whispers. They went a tortuous way through a district of fine residences where the close lights gleamed upon broad asphalt avenues; then the houses on both sides began to diminish in size and wealth. He left the wagon and went on at a walk.

The houses became smaller and humbler; he went by the shadowy walls of a gas tank, crossed a network of railway tracks, entered a narrow street lined with dingy cottages, and turned a corner. It was years since he had come this way, and then he had had a guide; but he had not forgotten a detail of the street. He went on without hesitation and knocked at the door of a small cottage, newly painted red. There was a long silence, then a stir, and the door opened. Tom Ryan faced him, Tom Ryan, the friend of his boyhood, with whom he had eaten shortly before his last arrest, the hod-carrier whose security, then, he had envied.

Tom Ryan's face was very white, and his face was no welcome. He stood at the door and stared with eyes that showed fear, at the man he had known in boyhood. Suddenly a gulp came in his throat. "Good God," he said, "you're not John Collins, John, are you? You're not John Collins, are you, John? Oh, my God!"

Collins caught the look, the fear, the shocked surprise. "Yes, it's me," he said, anger flaming through him. "What sort of a handout is this you're giving me? Do I get in?"

And roughly he pushed within. The door closed behind them; they were in the narrow hallway, which smelled of must and cookery. "Good God," muttered Ryan; "I didn't think you'd look like this; not like this!" Through the jar of the door at the bottom of the hall, with the stifling odor of a room at once kitchen and nursery, came a streak of yellow lamplight. In the faint glow the two men looked at each other, the hod-carrier with shoulders white with plaster and face white with emotion, the murderer with bloodshot eyes and corroded brow, his mouth like a straight blue scar. Ryan was trembling. "Man," he said, "what have you been doing! I never looked for anything like that when I told Nell I'd help ye!"

John Collins was silent for a moment; with a certain astonishment he saw the horror in the other's face. A scowl deepened his brows.

"Done!" he muttered. "Done—that's nothing to what I'll be doin' to ye if ye don't shut up that jaw of yours. Is that all ye've to say to me"—his voice rose—"is that all, eh? And Nell, where's Nell?"

A stir came from the room at the bottom of the hallway, then the thin wail of a baby. Ryan raised his hand.

"Sh-sh-sh," he hissed, and made a warning gesture. "Sh-sh-sh; the old woman, she don't know. I done it fer you— was willing you meet here. But I didn't know you'd do that, not that. And the papers full of it—I don't know—God help me," he ended with a groan.

"Where's Nell?" said Collins, and he shook Ryan by the shoulders; "where's Nell; quick; where's Nell?"

"She was to be here—let go, man, let go my shoulder— she's not come. Wish to God she had—I never knew 'twould come to this—be still—for God's sake don't go in there, not in there!"

But Collins, brushing him aside, had strode into the kitchen.

Mrs. Ryan was bending over the cradle—the same cradle where she had bent years before, and it was in the same corner, and from it came the acid cry of her last born. Side by side, by the cradle, were three cots; upon the pillows of

ch. ends p. 106

two were the grimy blond heads of two older children; but one child, the eldest, a girl, had fallen asleep in her chair; her head, pillowed on her arms, lay amid the unwashed dishes of the table, half-hidden by the large leaves of a newspaper sprawled loosely across.

"Sh-sh-sh, the babe, the babe," Mrs. Ryan was murmuring, holding up with her left hand a corner of a little blanket; and then, looking beneath her arm at the sound of entering feet, she caught sight of the sinister figure behind her. She whirled around, in one bound placed herself before the beds, her face lit up with a white ferocity; and she shot both clenched hands forward in a movement half sign of aversion, half blow. Collins shrank from the gesture.

"Go away," she cried, "from this room. Get out of sight of these children, you"—her breast swelled, then the words came slowly, drawn deep from her thick chest—"you murrdhering monster!"

Collins clenched his fist and scowled at Ryan, now come within the room. "Shut up that woman," he said.

Ryan went to his wife and placed his hand on her shoulder; but she stared straight ahead over his, at Collins, her breast heaving.

And on the table Collins saw the newspaper, an evening edition marked "Extra" in black affrighted letters, and across the page in great red letters was his name, and in a frame, the names of the men he had killed—five—and those he had wounded—three more.

"Ye murrdhering monster," panted Mrs. Ryan, following the movement of his eyes.

From the porch outside there came a faint shuffling of feet. Collins crouched, his hand went to his waistband, the heavy black revolver flew out. "One more sound," he said—and his voice became low with steady menace—"and I'll blow out the heads of every wan of you."

One of the children raised up in her cot; she gazed round-eyed at the strange man above her, and began to cry. Without changing her position, Mrs. Ryan dropped her hand and twined a curl about her finger in soothing caress. The child was stilled.

Collins scowled at them—at the mother, standing there, one hand soothing, her whole body tense before her children, a defense, a barrier; at the man, red-faced, perplexed, horror-stricken yet pitying; at the child up in its cot, at the child sleeping with its head among the dishes on the table. Then, warning them once more in terrible and grotesque pantomime with his revolver, he stepped backward through the door, which immediately slammed shut upon the group, petrified in bronze attitudes.

Out in the hallway, he wheeled and covered the outer door, which was opening. It shut again. A woman had come in. "Nell," he whispered.

She was by his side, in the darkness, putting something in his hand. "Quick!" she said.

He opened the box and dropped the rifle cartridges loose into his pocket. She gave him another one.

"Quick!" she said again; "the place's going to be shadowed."

He grasped the thing that she gave him.

"All I could get," she whispered; "all I could get; two years' stealin's."

It was a bundle of bank-notes. To the touch an old forgotten feeling swept hot through him. "Who's keepin' you? Who're you hanging up with?" he growled, his iron fingers sinking into her shoulder.

She was against him; in the semi-obscurity he could see her face, worn now; it was turned up to him wide-eyed.

"I couldn't do it alone, John," she said, in a wondering tone; "*I* couldn't climb walls and plant guns; I couldn't do *that*, John."

He thrust her aside and started for the door. Her two hands half went out after him in an unvoluntary detaining gesture, but "Quick," she whispered, fiercely; "quick, for the hills!"

ch. ends next p.

 9009

The door swept open; he plunged down the steps as if into a black sea; his feet did not sound; there was immediate silence.

"He's gone," she said, there alone, in the still dark hallway.

0015

Three weeks later, limping along a road a hundred and fifty miles south of the city, John Collins stopped, listened intently with frowning brows, and then, climbing up a bank, crawled into the chaparral and instantly fell asleep.

In three weeks he had gone a hundred and fifty miles in a straight line, but he had traveled probably a thousand—running, trotting, doubling, dodging, ambushing, killing. His goal had been to the east; time and time again he had made a desperate dash for the Sierra, snow-capped in the distance, the Sierra, with its profundity of forest, its intimacy of valleys, its secrecy of meadows, with its running water, its game, its sheep-herders, half-mad with solitude; and each time he had been headed off and slid on farther down the coast. But this morning he had seen before him a hill-range coming high-peaked to the sea; this was now his goal. From the place where he slept, the land fell off to the south in a broad valley golden-hazed at the bottom with unleafed willows, then rose again in long elastic jumps to a first crest, tumbled abruptly into a black canyon, and leaped up perpendicularly to a final summit dark with pines and promising of impenetrable recesses.

And behind him, to the north, men were hunting. For three weeks he had been pursued as a wild animal, with growing savagery of purpose, with increase of cunning, by greater numbers. The whole State, aroused, was buzzing about him like a beehive. Hundreds of men, armed as he was, clamored on his trail. Some had seen him; it was a sudden vision, instantaneous and flitting as the revelation of a photographer's flashlight—a grinning mask, a savage eye glinting along a rifle-barrel—and then men died, men with fingers upon triggers, before they could pull a trigger. The farmers in the fields worked with rifles in their hands, with pistols, with pitchforks; children armed with shotguns watched in the kitchens while their mothers cooked; the officers of five counties at the head of posses tracked him indefatigably; and leading them all was the best manhunter of the State—the grizzled, keen-eyed sheriff who, years before, had taken John Collins to prison. Twice, close-pressed Collins had seen him, with his broad sombrero, his black mustache, streaked with gray; but neither time had he had the chance to kill him.

The elements, also, had conspired against the fleeing convict.

For the first week, the drought had persevered. He had traveled through a parched and arid land. The sun poured like molten lead upon his bare head; dust lay about him like a suffocation; it piled on the roads, sifted through the holes in his shoes, burning his feet; it caked his dry lips; it inflamed his eyes; he had suffered thirst.

Then the long-delayed rains had come. The leaden vault of the sky had burst, letting down upon him the upper reservoirs. For a week he had been wet, persistently, all of the time; he had traveled in ooze; his clothes had clung cold about his limbs, paralyzing them; he had slept in puddles; and always, like a persecution with him, went the necessity of caring for his gun—of seeing that it be not wet, that it rust not, that it stay smoothly working, well-oiled, swiftly ready to kill.

He had borne these things with alacrity.[1] A feeling of phenomenal endurance had exalted him. All the time, in want, in hunger, in thirst, in heat or cold, in pursuit or short

---

[1] Liveliness; eagerness.

respite, killing or hiding, he had felt that he could go on thus forever; that his nerves were steel, his muscles iron, that nobody, nothing, God Himself, now could ever bring him down. When he shot, it was by reflex, with utmost surety, his game looming large as a mountain against the bead of his rifle.

But the last few days, something insidious had attacked him—something that he felt but vaguely, that he could not name, but which he distrusted profoundly.

A few days before, the rains had ceased, and the sun had shone again.

It shone through an air that was as old-gold dust, upon a wet land along the surface of which trailed silver hazes; upon a warm, moist land which panted to its touch, exhaling sighs humid and soft and fragrant as the breath of kine.[2] Overnight a giant painter seemed to work with broad sure brush. The landscape, yellow and smooth as if gold-lacquered at sunset, at sunrise was tinted in lavenders; the next morning it was light green; the next morning it was dark green; and in the fields, on the roads by the side of the ruts, at first a mere verdant mustiness, the grass was springing, numerous, strong and serried, as to the commanding stamp of some fantastic foot. Here and there, on some rounded hill, a plowman showed, a poster plowman behind four poster horses; he rolled up in his share, as though it were ribbon, long strips of emerald sward, turning up to the sun the deeper land, tinged with red, with the red of its proffered generous blood. A heaviness was in the air; at the slightest movement, sweat poured out upon Collins' body; a listlessness was in his limbs, a listlessness that was not unpleasant, but which worried him; his veins, swollen as were the streams, as were the budding twigs, ran with a torpor,[3] a peace almost, which he fought; at times a softness came to him, a vague mournfulness, which was not bitter, which was almost sweet, which relaxed his

---

[2] The archaic plural form of cows.

[3] A state of physical or mental inactivity; lethargy.

ch. ends p. 117

sinews, his nerves, his vigilance—his hate almost. It was something subtle and inexplicable, something at which he growled, but that he could not resist, something which he distrusted, but could not conquer.

And now it was with him as he slept, there in the chaparral, by the roadway. This it was which caused him to lie loosely asprawl on his back, his rifle almost beyond reach, his right arm across his eyes; it made him breathe deep; it lay about him like a warm soothing bath.

On the last day of the rain, by a cunning redoubled doubling, he had gained half a day on the leading posse, led by the sheriff. Since that, torpid with the new influence, he had been content to plod straight ahead, holding the gained advantage. This morning he had decided to give up two hours of it to sleep. He had lain down with the intention of sleeping two hours, fitfully, on the watch, like a dog, as was his way.

But now he was sleeping profoundly, on his back, his arm across his eyes, his rifle carelessly rolled ten feet away. An hour passed; he still slept. Another, and he still slept. A mile behind, a group of horsemen came along the road slowly.

Their eyes were bloodshot, the mud lay caked in the stubble of their unshaven faces, and they shifted uneasily in their deep saddles. Ahead, like a vedette,[4] scanning the way, rode a keen-eyed man, with dark mustache grayly streaked, a sombrero upon his grizzled head. He bent low, along the flank of his horse, stopped the animal, bent lower, looking into the drying mud of the road, then spoke a few muttered words to the men who now were about him. Immediately they tensed; weariness fled them. And John Collins, in the brush a mile ahead, became fitful in his sleep.

The horses raised their heads to the reins and began to trot. The riders, rising in their saddles, looked ahead, their rifles in their right hands ready for use. An animal stumbled

---

[4] A soldier on horseback positioned beyond an army's outposts to observe the movements of the enemy.

in the rear; the rider cursed, and the sheriff silenced him with a potent look. They were within half a mile of the sleeper now; he awoke suddenly.

He awoke, listened, then crept through the brush to the summit of a little knoll and looked.

He saw them—the sheriff and his posse—coming down the road. He looked toward the east, up the valley; from this direction another group of horsemen was approaching. The two posses were drawing an angle of which he was the apex. And three miles away to the south lay the mountains, black with pines, impenetrable to search; he had slept at their very feet while the hunters came upon him. He cursed—but even as he cursed a subtle indifference, a carelessness, was within him.

A short distance ahead of the point where he now stood, between it and the posse coming slowly down the valley, a fainter road crossed toward the hills he sought. At a bend, in a little hollow shaded by a live-oak, a mossy watering-trough dripped, and toward the trough a boy was riding at a walk, on a young horse, bareback. Bending low, Collins glided through the brush, down the hillside, and gained a patch of woods that, paralleling the main road along which the two posses were converging, extended to the trough. He stepped out of the fringe of willows just as the boy brought his horse to a stop beneath the live-oak. Men's voices came to him from the junction of the roads, one hundred yards away; the posse from up the valley was passing it.

The boy, startled, threw his eyes toward the crackling twigs and looked into the muzzle of the rifle. "Get off that horse," Collins said, and took a step toward the trough.

The boy slid to the ground along the horse's gleaming flank; the man, watching him narrowly, his rifle at the hip, lowered his head and drank.

A shout came from the road. The two posses had met. Voices mingled in surprise; then in loud discussion. Collins took a step backward into the willows.

ch. ends p. 117

"Where's water in them hills?" he asked the boy, jerking his thumb toward the mountains across the valley, to the south.

The boy pointed to a rounded summit, crowned with black pines, across the valley, to the south.

Collins raised his rifle, clubbed. He knew that he must kill the boy; all through his flight this had been his rigid line of conduct: to kill those from whom he obtained information according to which he must act.

But now, at this moment of peril, with the voices of the posses floating clear to him on the quiet air, the feeling that had been with him since the cessation of the rain enwrapped him subtly—an indifference it was, a weariness, a laziness—he didn't know what it was; but it made him say:

"If I don't kill you, will you keep still?"

The boy nodded mutely.

A grimace suddenly distended the fugitive's cracked face, a strange grimace, like the decrepit contortion of what might once have been a smile; and his eyes lit up, lit up with something that might have been the shadow of a softness. "Cross your heart and die?" he asked.

The boy crossed his heart, his staring face very serious.

Collins leaped upon the horse and was off.

He did not ride toward the mountain to which the boy had pointed. He turned his back to it, made for the main road down which had passed the second posse, swung into it, and went up the valley, at right angles to the course that would take him to his goal. As he turned into the main road, a yell had sounded. Another rose now; a rifle cracked. He had been seen by some member of the posses. He rounded a sharp double-turn beneath the branches of a sycamore which scraped him as he passed, and a long ribbon of road stretched level before him. The horse was young and fresh; Collins bent forward, his face almost between its ears, and to his mutter it leaped in great bounds. Behind, the yells ceased; they were superseded by a drumming of hoofs, steady, constant like a buzzing; at times bullets cried wild overhead.

The planking of a bridge reverberated hollow beneath him; he rounded another turn. This time, when he had gone three hundred yards beyond it, he brought his horse up in three short cow-pony jumps, wheeled it around at a stand, raised his rifle, and waited for the first man to make the turn.

It was as he had expected. The first horseman was the sheriff; riding strongly but calmly, the rim of his sombrero blowing back, his face very grim. Collins held the bead of his rifle against him longer than was necessary (all through his flight he had fired from all angles, in all positions, with absolute accuracy); he chuckled as he pulled the trigger; then, without waiting to look, whirled his horse under him and sprang forward again.

After a while, looking beneath his armpit, he saw vaguely a man riding after him, a man with a sombrero. He turned and looked fair. It was the sheriff, riding strongly but calmly, his sombrero rim flapping, his face very grim; he had missed the sheriff.

It was the first time since he had the rifle that he had missed. Heretofore the gun had leaped to his hip, to his shoulder, by reflex and had blazed death always. It had been impossible to miss; in his eyes the game had loomed up like a mountain. And now he had missed. A fear came upon him; a fear as of the supernatural; clubbing his horse with the butt of the faithless weapon he urged it forward at greater speed; it was beginning to pant now.

The road was rising with the floor of the valley. Ahead on either side lay half-plowed fields; he saw men bent over their plows behind four-horse teams. One of the teams stopped abruptly; the plowman ran to his horses, fumbled at the traces. Another man, to the left, was doing the same thing. And then, from each arrested plow with its drooping-headed animals, a horse detached itself, traces dragging loose behind, the plowman on its back, and loped with lumbering steps toward the road. And Collins caught a glint of shotgun barrels. A shout came from behind; Collins turned his head;

three more ponderous beasts, mounted by farmers lustful for the hunt, were coming across the fields, traces flying behind, spurning with their broad hoofs shining clods. Again he struck his horse with the butt of his rifle—and the breath began to whistle in its throat. A bullet snarled by, close to his head; from the upper window of a farmhouse a shotgun bellowed. He passed a schoolhouse; he saw the children, released for recess, swarm out of the doors like bees; he glimpsed their white faces; their shrill cries came to him in one brief note as he swept by, and then he swerved to the left into a road that went through a pasture and then on toward the mouth of a canyon. He had to open a gate; he fought at it long, it seemed, but when remounting, he cast a look backward, he saw the winded plow horses still toiling up the hill, and behind them, strung out, the two posses. Behind, there were more horsemen; and to the right and the left, horsemen; the whole world seemed aroused, converging upon him. He picked up his sagging beast between his knees, and galloped into the dusk of the canyon.

It led away from the hill he had for goal. He went on half a mile, left his horse in the brush, went on afoot another half mile, leaving a fairly visible but diminishing trail, then, crawling through the underbrush, doubled back along the walls of the canyon, toward the south.

Crawling, springing from stone to stone, always in the brush, covering his rare tracks carefully, he climbed diagonally up across the face of the hills for several hours; and the afternoon sun struck him in a warm wave as at last he came out upon a round plateau, crowned with a circle of black pines; running to the center, he thrust his face into the cool tufts of watercress and drank, in long sucking gulps, like a horse. The boy had told him right.

When he had quenched his thirst to some degree, he stood up and listened, intent. A quiet was about him, a great golden quiet; a little bird went by his head with a squeak and a whir, and the silence came flowing back in long ripples, like a sea. It was the silence of altitudes, vibrant, supersensitive, through which a sound passed aquiver like a pain; along its crystal, a whisper, a mutter, the crackling of a twig, would come for a mile. Collins listened: there was no crackling of twig, no shout, no cry, not a breath, not a sigh.

He walked to the edge of the plateau and looked down the slopes to the valley beneath. Along the ribbon of road, small like mice, and gliding without rise and fall as upon wheels, he saw specks of horses mounted by dots of men; they were going up and down the road in sudden swift flights, as if bewildered. He had outwitted them.

He returned, dragging his rifle, a little aimlessly to the center of the plateau. He knew what he should do—plunge on into the depths of the mountains rising and falling ahead to the south, dark with pines. But a laziness, almost an indifference, possessed him—the strange influence that had been with him since the ceasing of the rain. It had left him in the excitement of the chase; now it was with him again, a vague weariness, an indolence. He looked about him. The plateau, ringed with a circle of pines, fell off toward the center in a gentle depression. In the depression was the spring, bubbling up silvery among the cress. The little stream wound lazily for a few feet, then tumbled abruptly over a mossy log in miniature cataract. About it the grass was lush and high, and in the grass flowers peeped—pink flowers, like small roses, and blue ones, like eyes. The grass looked very thick and very soft. He sat down.

And then immediately, sudden as a blow, there came to him the realization that he was outside. He was out in the open.

He had been out for three weeks; three weeks before he had passed forever outside of the prison's gray walls. During that time he had traveled, he had fought; he had slept in the rain, he had slept under the stars; the sun had poured upon him, the wind had slashed him; not once had he been under

ch. ends next p.

a roof. And now, for the first time, he realized that he was outside.

He realized the golden stream of sunlight slanting to him across the hills, the smell of fresh earth, of lush grass; he breathed deep and felt within his lungs the clean clear air of out of doors; he saw the sky above him.

It was blue, the sky, a fresh tender blue. And right at its highest point, overhead, was a little white cloud. He let himself fall back, and lay there, eyes up. The little white cloud receded, receded, seemed about to withdraw within a secret door, up there in the blue dome. He shut his eyes; when he reopened them, the little cloud was again in its place.

A bee buzzed by—an hour passed. A golden spider weaved a fragile net from one blade of grass to another.

A soft drum of hoofs on the sward threw him sitting up, his hand on his rifle. At the edge of the meadow a colt stood regarding him obliquely, half-scared, its long knobbed fore-legs far apart. "Phoo!" said Collins. With a defiant flip of hind-heels, the colt vanished down the slope.

Collins remained thus, seated, rifle in hand, a moment. His movement at the approach of the colt had been slow; now a languor was in him—in his limbs, in his veins, a heavy languor, rather pleasant. He lay down again and gazed up at the little white cloud. It retreated within the depths of the heavens. He shut his eyes. It sprang forth again, playfully.

And meanwhile a posse was laboriously climbing toward the rounded hill crowned with pines. It filed up slowly, in long zigzags. At its head was the sheriff, patient and grim; he was guided by the boy whom Collins had met at the watering-trough.

The posse debouched[5] upon the plateau, and quietly, following the gestured commands of the sheriff, the men scattered in a circle behind the pines crowning it.

One of the men stepped upon a dry twig, and Collins sat up to the crackle. He saw the man, dodging behind a tree,

---

[5] Emerged from a narrow or confined space into a wide, open area.

and at the same time, another, then arms passing or faces peering from behind other trees. He grasped his rifle and half stood up.

He remained thus, on his knee, a moment; he seemed listening intently, listening not to what might come from the outside, but to some subtle inner command. And a great wave of lassitude, of the inexplicable lassitude that for several days had lurked about him, now whelmed him in a long, heavy and enveloping caress.

"Oh, hell!" he said—and he lay down again on his back, in the lush grass, and gazed up at the little white cloud far up in the blue sky, the fresh tender blue sky.

And to the sheriff's raised ordering hand, the manhunters began to shoot. They shot from a circle, at the stretched figure in the center. It was hidden by the grass, it lay flat, it was a hard shot; the thing took a long time. Bullets spattered all about Collins; after a while one went through his left arm, which lay across his chest. To the sting he rose, half angrily, and made a movement toward his rifle, then, "Oh, hell!" he said again, with heavy indifference.

It was almost sundown when the wily old sheriff, taught by many lessons the futility of haste, ordered a concentric advance. The men rushed forward; they met face to face above a lifeless body.

The sheriff touched it lightly with the tip of his boot. "Well," he said, and his low voice in the still air had an unexpected, booming finality; "well, he *was* a bad one."

But John Collins, with glazed eyes, was staring up at the cloud.

The Tracy-Merrill Escape

from
Sensational Prison Escapes
from the Oregon State Penitentiary
by
Prisoner #6435

SENSATIONAL OUTBREAK AT THE STATE PRISON

Three Guards Killed by Two Desperate Convicts Early Yesterday Morning and the Murderers Scaled the Wall and Made Their Escape.

Harry Tracy and David Merrill, the Two Slayers of Their Keepers, Make a Daring Effort to Secure Their Liberty, and Succeed in Getting Away—Posses Are on the Hunt for the Men—Wanton Killing of Frank B. Ferrell, S. R. T. Jones and B. T. Tiffany.

Salem was thrown into a fever of ex-   suit of the two murderers—about fifty

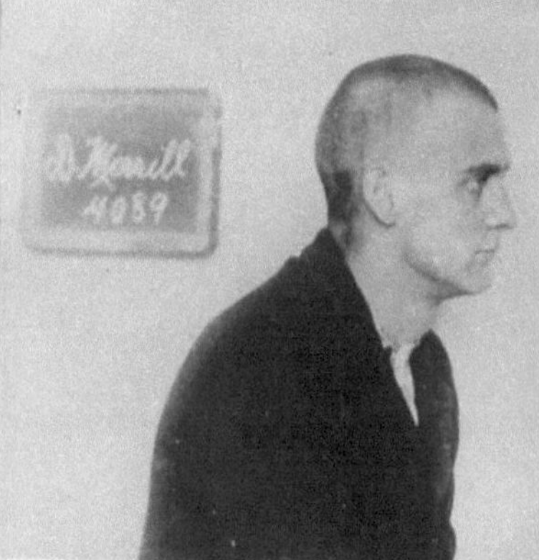

Prisoner Wearing Metal Boot Can't Escape

DANGEROUS criminals, shackled with a metal "Oregon" boot, have little chance to escape during long railway journeys. The boot, a modern adaptation of the old-fashioned ball and chain, consists of a steel framework fitting over the shoe, with a 50-pound collar above the ankle.

The prisoner who wears it can walk slowly with a fair degree of comfort, but should he attempt to run, or move quickly, the heavy weight will break his leg.

TRACY'S LAST FIGHT

The Outlaw Was Surrounded in a Barn on the Eddy Farm.

(Journal Special Service.)

SPOKANE, Wash., Aug. 6.—Harry Tracy killed himself about 11 last night by firing a bullet through his brain.

As soon as young Goldfinch brought word to Creston that Tracy was at the Eddy farm, a posse of citizens quickly left for the scene of the outlaw's last exploit.

The Tracy-Merrill Escape

On the 22nd day of March, 1899, Harry Tracy, prison number 4088, and David Merrill, prison number 4089, were received at the Oregon State Penitentiary from Multnomah County, where they were sentenced for assault and robbery.

Tracy was born in Wisconsin; was twenty-four years of age, 5 feet 8 inches in height, and had previously served a term in the Utah State Penitentiary.

Merrill was a native of Washington, age 28, height 5 feet 8 inches, with a previous record in the Oregon State Penitentiary as number 2314.

Tracy was under sentence of twenty years and Merrill thirteen years. Their escape was made on the 9th day of June, 1902, just three years and 77 days after their arrival. So much for prison statistics.

Their conduct as prisoners was bad and only a short time after their receipt they began to cause the prison officials constant trouble, and are said to have been ironed with "Oregon boots" [1] and closely watched. The escape which took place on the morning of the date named followed an excursion to Salem on the day before, during which the party or parties

---

[1] The Oregon Boot, or Gardner Shackle as it was properly known, was patented July 3, 1866, by J.C. Gardner, warden of Oregon State Penitentiary.

9009

who placed the guns and ammunition in the molding room are supposed to have reached Salem, and under cover of darkness scaled the prison walls and placed them where they were found by Tracy.

Only someone who was familiar with the prison and knew its inside workings and Tracy's place in the molding room could have succeeded in escaping the guard patrol and have carried out the plans so well.

That the escape was well planned is evident. Tracy for some time prior to the escape had been studying a map of Oregon and thoroughly familiarized himself with roads, trails, towns, etc., on the route over which he afterward passed. That he had been expecting outside help for some time is shown by the fact that for several weeks prior to that memorable morning he would, upon entering the molding room to begin work, hasten at once to his floor and search among the boxes and under the dust paper with which it was supplied. Although no particular attention was paid to his actions at the time, after his escape they were recalled and spoken of by prisoners who worked on adjoining floors.

Tracy and his associate in the escape, Merrill, were cellmates and were also employed on the same floor. It is supposed they induced some ex-convict with whom they had been familiar, to return and bring the firearms with which they made their escape.

A year or two later it developed that a former convict, Charles Monte by name, who served time with Tracy and Merrill, and was quite intimate with them, had made the boast that he was the party who had scaled the walls and placed guns and ammunition in a place previously designated where they would eventually be found by the right parties. Monte was arrested, tried and convicted, and on July 15, 1905, was sentenced to life imprisonment. His boasting nature and desire to show off as a "bad man from Bitter Creek," fell to zero when a life jolt[2] was handed him, and

---

[2] Prison slang for a long sentence.

at the time much doubt was expressed as to his ability and nerve to pull off such a stunt. To know the man—nothing but a boastful, whining mongrel—was to immediately become convinced that he was utterly incapable of such a deed of daring. However he was kept in confinement over nine years before he was released, a sadder but not much wiser man.

To describe the escape by all the reports which have been given by "eyewitnesses" would be a big task. What follows is about as near the truth as is possible to get it from the maze of conflicting stories told:

Prisoners were counted as they lined up to march to the shops. The count had just been made. Tracy and Merrill were at or near the head of the line which contained something like 150 prisoners. As they entered the molding room Tracy went at once to his floor, as was his custom, and searching there found the guns. Taking up a Winchester he threw the lever and raising it to his shoulder fired at and killed the molding room guard, Mr. Ferrell, who was standing with his back toward him just a short distance away.

Mr. Ferrell, who was pacing, as was his custom, on the walk leading to the other departments, lived only an instant after being shot. Tracy, reloading his rifle, is said to have went toward the murdered guard far enough to note the effect of his shot, and then, with Merrill, who had secured the other rifle to assist him, he ordered the other prisoners into an opposite part of the molding room.

He then went to a window facing on the front yard and began firing at the guards in post number one. After firing several shots he and Merrill made their way through into the front shops. After passing through an alleyway leading into the adjoining department they were encountered by a prisoner who was shot, it is said, in trying to wrest the gun from Tracy's hands. After this shooting they made their way through the front shop and, securing a ladder in the carpenter shop, came out on the opposite side of the shops and facing the west wall.

ch. ends p. 130

As they emerged from the building, screened by piles of old boxes then standing there, and which served as a shield, they began firing at the guards occupying towers commanding a view of that portion of the yard. Mr. Tiffany, who had been occupying the northeast corner tower, had been transferred to a position as turnkey in the warden's office, was present on the wall explaining guard duties to his successor, Mr. Ross, when the shooting began. As the outlaws emerged from the shop and commenced to fire from their hidden position behind the boxes, Mr. Ross, to whom he had handed his rifle, was struck by one of the shots and knocked from the wall path on which the guards patrol. Mr. Tiffany, to secure the gun which had fallen to the ground, jumped from the wall, intending to secure it and return to guard that portion of the wall.

In the meantime, Tracy and Merrill, supposing most likely that they had killed or badly wounded the guards in the vacant tower, but unable to silence the rifle fire from the tower on their right, turned to the left, and still keeping behind the boxes which screened them made their way toward the north wall. Occasionally the guard would see them as they passed through an opening, but although he fired several shots and stood bravely on the wall, exposed to dangerous rifle fire, could not get a successful shot.

After reaching the end of the shop buildings the outlaws turned, and still protected by a corner of the building around which they passed, crossed to the wall. As they reached it, placing the ladder, one of them stood guard while the other passed to the top of the wall. In nearing the wall they had come out in plain sight of the guard occupying the northwest corner tower.

This guard, Mr, Jones, who was killed, looking for the escapees elsewhere and guarding the front portion of the prison yard, was watching in a partly exposed position, and is said to have been shot from the wall.

Reaching the ground on the outside of the enclosure,

Tracy and Merrill then turned and following along the wall in an easterly direction turned the corner and came upon two guards who were then making their way back to remount the wall. Before they were seen they had them covered and ordered them to throw up their hands and march. Using them as a shield to protect them from the rifle fire of the guard in the tower they had been unable to silence, and within range of which they had again come, they passed to a position of safety and then ordered the guards to return. As they started to do so, Mr. Tiffany was shot in the back and killed in the same cold-blooded manner as was Mr. Ferrell.

The entire break, from the time the first shot was fired, to Mr. Tiffany's death did not consume more than five minutes.

The warden and his assistant, who often stood discussing the day's procedure and details of prison management for some time after the line had passed, were yet standing where they had stood to count when the first firing began.

Hastening at once to the house, the warden gave the alarm. Guards were armed and sent out and deputy warden, Mr. Ad Dilly, armed with a Winchester rifle, ran the full length of that portion of the prison wall leading from the prison buildings to the tower in which guard Jones, whom he had seen fall, lay dying. The escape by this time had been effected and the outlaws were gone.

When particulars of the state of affairs in the molding room had been obtained (it is said by telephone from the office) a prisoner carrying a flag of truce was sent from the house to the shops to give medical attention, and to also lead the prisoners back to the house, where they were counted and locked in their cells.

The wounded prisoner, almost dead from the loss of blood, was carried hastily to the hospital, where measures were taken to arrest the flow. Afterward one of his legs, badly shattered by the discharging rifle in his encounter with Tracy, was amputated above the knee, and still later he was pardoned.

ch. ends p. 130

Tracy, who was a dead shot in the exact meaning of the word, set the whole country by the ears, until it was "Tracy mad." With the coolest kind of dime-novel daring he escaped time and again from apparently absolute traps, only to show up a few days later after some new adventure and repeat the performance.

His trail led through Salem, Portland, and Seattle, finally running eastward toward the Hole-in-the-Wall country, which he never reached.

All along the way he spread terror among the country-folk, often walking into a farmhouse behind a gun and demanding food, and in one instance kidnapping a swede farmhand whom he held for several days as a personal servant.

His duel with Merrill and the slaughter of three men in battle with peace officers and newspaper men near Seattle were the great outstanding features of the chase.

About the latter end of June, he and Merrill, then together in the State of Washington, had a quarrel of some kind and agreed to fight out their differences with rifles. They were to walk a certain distance apart and then turn and fire. Tracy did not keep faith with Merrill, and turning, shot and killed him as he was walking away. However, when the body supposed to be Merrill's, whom, report said, Tracy had slain, was brought back to prison, many of the men seeing it, were quite positive that the remains were those of someone else than Merrill. Joseph "Bunko" Kelly, who had charge of the bathroom for many years, and who had seen Merrill stripped many times, tried to point out the error, but the body was in such decomposition that it was extremely difficult to make positive identification. The question as to the actual killing of Merrill by Tracy will, in all probabilities, remain forever unanswered. However, this is getting ahead of the story.

A posse of forty officers was formed and almost immediately the word was sent out that the escaped convicts were trapped in a wooded place halfway between Salem and the reform school.

But not so. That night, while officers watched the woods, the convicts appeared in Salem, stopped J. W. Roberts on the street, took his clothing and sent him on in his underwear, stole a team, and drove away. Bloodhounds were rushed from the penitentiary at Walla Walla, Washington. They came and hounded, but did no greater service than to encourage the morale of the posses with strenuous baying.

The following day this word came from Gervais, Oregon: "Tracy and Merrill were observed in a wheat field of Ellis Young near the Samuel Brown place at 2:45 this afternoon. Company D of Woodburn has arrived. The guards are closing in. The crisis is at hand."

But not so. The next day in the early morning the convicts appeared at the cabin of August King, a woodcutter, living near Gervais. They walked in and took some bread. Tracy didn't eat much. He rolled a cigarette then threw it away in disgust.

This, of course, gave a new clue, and a posse of 200 started on the trail. Meantime the convicts had doubled back, and robbed Dr. C. S. White of a coat and a horse and buggy and disappeared again.

The next seen of them was near Gervais when Charles Tuh, a guard, saw them climb over a fence. He shot and missed. The men then turned up for breakfast at the home of A. Akers, near Monitor, and again dropped from sight.

June 13—The chase was simply a blind search.

June 14—The posses were called off.

June 16—Tracy and Merrill passed through Portland, probably on a trolley, held up three men on the south bank of the Columbia, made them furnish dinner and ferry them across the river to the Washington side. There they held up another farmer, took the clothes off the back of a second

ch. ends p. 130

rancher whom they bound and gagged and fled into the timber back of Vancouver.

June 17—In a midnight fight with Bert Biesecker and Lon Davis, deputy sheriffs, Biesecker took a bullet through the coat sleeve. It was almost the only time Tracy ever fired and missed.

June 18—They appeared at LaCenter.

June 19—They appeared at a farmhouse three miles from LaCenter, demanded food and disappeared again. About this time the convicts were forced to give way in public interest to King Edward VII of England, whose illness, it was feared, might prevent his coronation. The king got well.

July 3—Tracy appeared alone near Lake Washington. He told persons whom he forced to serve him with food that he had killed Merrill near Chehalis. "I was tired of him, anyhow," he said.

The same day, Tracy ran into a posse that included Deputy Sheriffs Raymond, Bower, and Williams, Karl Anderson, then a reporter for the *Seattle Times*, now assistant managing editor of the *San Francisco Chronicle*, and Louis B. Sefrit, another newspaperman. The clash occurred two miles from Bothel.

Tracy killed Raymond, Bower, and Williams. Anderson fired three shots at Tracy and himself escaped death by a miracle. The governor of Washington called out the national guard.

Two days later, Tracy forced a Japanese man to ferry him across from Port Madison and disappeared on a nautical junket on the sound. On Bainbridge Island he kidnapped John Anderson, a Swede farm hand and took him along as his personal flunky.

July 9—Tracy and Merrill were both reported surrounded at Orollia, although Merrill was dead at the time. Again capture seemed certain.

But not so. The next day Tracy made a farmer named Johnson go to Tacoma and buy a revolver and some ammunition for him on threat of murdering Johnson's whole family.

July 11—Tracy broke through another cordon after a hot but bloodless fight near Covington.

Hounds found a new trail. It was reported that Merrill had shown up at Ravensdale and that Tracy was organizing a gang which he intended to head as a second Jesse James.

July 14—Tracy had outwitted his pursuers again and lost himself. A reward of $6,000 was offered. [3]

July 15—Merrill's body was found near Chehalis by a woman and her son picking blackberries.

July 17—Tracy was again reported in a trap—and out again.

Then for a time Tracy dropped out of the public eye until the matter of the Fitzsimmons-Jeffries fight had been settled. [4]

July 23—Tracy, looking fresh and rested, ate breakfast in the vicinity of Palmer. It was the first seen of him in days. Apparently he had been resting and taking in the news of the fight.

---

[3] Adjusted for inflation, $6,000 in 1902 would be equivalent to approximately $200,000 in 2022.

[4] Professional American boxer James J. Jeffries (1875–1953), known as "The Boilermaker" and once considered one of the greatest Heavyweight Champions of all time, won the world heavyweight title in 1899 from British boxer Bob "The Fighting Blacksmith" Fitzsimmons (1863–1917), boxing's first three-division world champion. Three years later, on July 25, 1902, a rematch took place. After Bob "inexplicably" lowered his guard, Jeffries knocked him out cold in round eight.

ch. ends next p.

August 1—Tracy crossed the Columbia into Eastern Washington carrying four guns and 200 rounds of ammunition. He was headed for the Hole-in-the-Wall.

August 5—C. V. Drazon, a farmer living near Odessa, Washington, found this note pinned on his door:

"To Whom It May Concern: Tell Mr. Cudihee [the sheriff of King County, Washington], to take a tumble and let me alone or I will fix him plenty. I will be on my way to Wyoming. If your horses was any good would swap with you. Thanks for a cool drink.
"HARRY TRACY."

The next day was the last for Tracy. But they did not take him alive. The first brief flash from Spokane read:

"Tracy's race is run. The notorious outlaw killed himself last night by shooting with a revolver."

He had been wounded in the right leg between the knee and thigh in a battle with a posse under Sheriff Gardner. He committed suicide twenty minutes after being wounded. His body was found at daybreak that morning in a wheat field, the revolver tightly grasped in his right hand.

HONORARY HEATHEN

"well, he *was* a bad one."